THE ODDS

The townspeople began to run for cover, seeking a safe place to watch the action. J.T. watched the men as they positioned themselves. Parker was on the far right, Reeves on the left and McAlester in the middle, McAlester wore two colt .44's in crisscrossed gun belts. Pushing the front of his duster back behind the grips, he set his feet a narrow distance apart. The sign of a man who had found himself in similar situations before.

"You must think you're pretty damn good with that iron, mister. Takin' on three guns, I'd say you're bitin' off a damn big chew," said McAlester.

"Yeah," said Parker, "What name you want these Mex to put on your tombstone?"

"Law—John Thomas Law," came the reply.

"J. T. Law," uttered Harry Reeves. "We're dead . . ."

DON'T MISS THESE
ALL-ACTION WESTERN SERIES
FROM THE BERKLEY PUBLISHING GROUP

THE GUNSMITH by J. R. Roberts
Clint Adams was a legend among lawmen, outlaws and ladies. They called him . . . the Gunsmith.

LONGARM by Tabor Evans
The popular long-running series about Deputy U.S. Marshal Long—his life, his loves, his fight for justice.

SLOCUM by Jake Logan
Today's longest-running action Western. John Slocum rides a deadly trail of hot blood and cold steel.

BUSHWHACKERS by B. J. Lanagan
An action-packed series by the creators of Longarm! The rousing adventures of the most brutal gang of cutthroats ever assembled—Quantrill's Raiders.

DIAMONDBACK by Guy Brewer
Dex Yancey is Diamondback, a Southern gentleman turned con man when his brother cheats him out of the family fortune. Ladies love him. Gamblers hate him. But nobody pulls one over on Dex. . . .

WILDGUN by Jack Hanson
The blazing adventures of mountain man Will Barlow—from the creators of Longarm!

TEXAS TRACKER by Tom Calhoun
Meet J. T. Law: the most relentless—and dangerous—manhunter in all Texas. Where sheriffs and posses fail, he's the best man to bring in the most vicious outlaws—for a price.

TEXAS TRACKER

GUNFIGHT AT
SANTA ANGELA

TOM CALHOUN

JOVE BOOKS, NEW YORK

This is a work of fiction. Names, characters, places, and incidents either are the product of the author's imagination or are used fictitiously, and any resemblance to actual persons, living or dead, business establishments, events, or locales is entirely coincidental.

GUNFIGHT AT SANTA ANGELA

A Jove Book / published by arrangement with
the author

PRINTING HISTORY
Jove edition / February 2003

Copyright © 2003 by Penguin Putnam Inc.
Cover design by Steven Ferlauto

Visit our website at
www.penguinputnam.com

ISBN: 0-515-13469-4

A JOVE BOOK®
Jove Books are published by The Berkley Publishing Group,
a division of Penguin Putnam Inc.,
375 Hudson Street, New York, New York 10014.
JOVE and the "J" design
are trademarks belonging to Penguin Putnam Inc.

PRINTED IN THE UNITED STATES OF AMERICA

10 9 8 7 6 5 4 3 2 1

ONE

★

IT WAS A hot day in mid-July when John Thomas Law, gunfighter and bounty hunter, brought his big roan to a halt at the cut-bank of the Concho River—or rather, what had been the Concho River. For now, it was nothing but a wide ditch filled with dry sand, much like most of the tributaries of the state caught up in the grip of the worst drought in the last twenty years.

Staring across to the other bank, Law watched a column of dust-covered black cavalrymen and their tired horses slowly making their way toward Fort Concho, the military post located only a mile or so farther up river. The unit was the famed 10th U.S. Cavalry, an all black trooper outfit known as "Buffalo Soldiers," a title bestowed upon them by one of the most ruthless and

worthy adversaries of the American plains—the Co-
manche Indian.

Watching the dust of the last passing trooper drift
away, John Law crossed the riverbed and rode toward
the town that was visible in the distance. This was
Santa Angela, a onetime trading post that had been
established at the same time Fort Concho was being
built. Within weeks of completion of the fort, Santa
Angela had gone from a small trading post to a full-
blown town almost overnight. Tents and storefronts appeared from out of nowhere, forming the first street. In
those early days the town's stock in trade was whiskey
and women. Saloons, gambling halls and whorehouses
made up most of the town, and the money flowed, not
only from the soldiers at the fort, but from the cowboys
and miners from the surrounding areas as well.

Over the last few years, legitimate merchants and
businessmen had moved into town, bringing with them
their wives and children. As the community had begun
to grow, civic-minded citizens soon brought pressure
to bear on the multitude of saloon owners and madams,
until finally only three saloons and a single whorehouse
were all that remained of a once thriving den of iniq-
uity. Those that had survived did so only because they
were deemed a necessary evil that provided a steady
cash flow to the community.

It had been five years since John Law had last been
through Santa Angela. There had been considerable
changes in that time, but from what he saw as he rode
the main street, those changes had been for the good.
The town, like most in Texas in the year 1877, was a
town on the rise. Besides the three saloons, there were

now two hotels, two general stores, a barbershop, a lawyer and doctor's office and a café. Off on a side street he saw the frameworks for a new church and a school that were in the early building stages.

Scattered out behind the stores on the right were dozens of adobes, signifying the town's Mexican populace. Behind the stores on the left were the fine wood-frame homes of the town's local merchants and businessmen. Some things would never change, thought J.T. as he headed for the livery at the end of the street. The gringos hired the Mexicans to clean their fine houses and to wash their clothes, but when the sun set, they were expected to stay in their own part of town. Law knew that among the many adobes he saw scattered out behind the town he would find a small town within a town. There he would find two or three cantinas that served the finest tequila and some of the best Mexican food in Texas.

Just as the Mexicans were expected to remain among their own, so were the black soldiers. Few, if any, ever ventured into the saloons or the café along Santa Angela's main street, but rather, they spent their free time and their money in the cantinas of the Mexican town, where they were more readily accepted. This didn't bother the white business owners at all. They still got the soldiers' money through the Mexicans, without having to actually deal with the black soldiers. There were two main reasons for this diverse arrangement, and both were the result of a deep underlying resentment that worked against the Mexican populace and the men of the 10th Calvary. Those two things were the Alamo and the Civil War. Texans weren't forgiving—and they damn sure weren't going to forget.

The tall, dark-haired stranger hardly drew a glance from the few people on the street. It was already well over a hundred degrees and most people were staying inside, out of the heat and the ever-present dust that was stirred by the occasional breeze.

Having walked the big roan to the end of town, John Law reined him in at the livery. Stepping down, he arched his back and stretched his saddle-weary body. An old Mexican man with hair and a goatee the color of fresh fallen snow ambled out of the barn. Looking up at the tall gringo with the blue-green eyes he asked, "How long you stay, *señor*?"

"One day, maybe two."

"Five dollars a day."

J.T. cocked his head to the side. "Kinda high for a livery ain't it, ol' man?"

The old man shrugged his stooped shoulders then pointed to the mountains to the west.

"*Sí, señor*. Only a small portion of that is to feed and stable your fine animal. The rest is for the water. I have to haul my water wagon thirty miles to those mountains and back to provide that service. Santa Angela's wells and the Concho dried up long ago. It is hard work, *señor*, and I am old, but your horse will be grateful for my trouble. I am sure."

J.T. pulled a five-dollar gold piece from his vest pocket and flipped it to the old man. "Well, in that case, I'd say you got a well-deserved five dollars comin' from me and a thank-you from my horse."

The old man snatched the gold piece out of the air and smiled.

"*Gracias, señor.* He will be well taken care of—you have my word."

J.T. nodded, then pulled his Winchester from the saddle boot. Untying his saddlebags and bedroll, he tossed them over his shoulder and walked up the street toward one of the hotels. Passing one of the saloons, he was tempted to go inside for a drink. After having ridden fifty miles, the taste of dust and alkaline was strong in his mouth. But as tempting as the thought of a drink might be, the idea of a room with a real bed was a stronger temptation. Beside, he had a bottle of whiskey in his saddlebags.

The hotel clerk was a short, bald man with a mustache. J.T. found him in a chair behind the counter, cocked back against the wall with his feet propped up on a desk. He was snoring. A sign hung next to the row of keys. "No Baths! No Water!" Ignoring the ledger that lay open on the counter, J.T. reached over and took a key from a hook only inches above the man's head. Going up the stairs, he found the room at the end of the hall. Inside there was a bed and a small table with a pitcher and a basin. On the other side of the bed was another small table that held a kerosene lamp. It wasn't the fancy Cattlemen's Hotel in Austin that he was used to, but for now this would do just fine.

He set his rifle in the corner near the door, then tossed the bedroll and saddlebags to the floor next to the bed and sat down. The well-worn mattress sagged under the weight of his solid two hundred pounds, but it was still better than the rock-hard ground he had been sleeping on the last two weeks. Finding a glass next to

the pitcher, he blew the dust out of it, lifted the pitcher
and poured. The water had a brown tint to it as it filled
the glass. That didn't matter—it was wet and it went
down smooth. A second glass took the dust out of his
mouth and eased his parched throat.

He poured water into the basin and set it on the floor
between his feet. Leaning forward, he bathed his deep
tanned face and the back of his neck. The water felt
good, reviving him, if only for a few minutes. The
thought of a bath crossed his mind, but the sign down-
stairs said it all. Right now, the ol' Mex at the livery
had more water than the whole town. That was probably where the brown water he had just drunk had
come from.

Removing his vest and shirt, he tossed them to the
end of the bed. Dipping his big hands into the basin
again, he splashed water onto his chest and under his
arms. For his efforts to cool down he was rewarded by
a short, but strong breeze that blew through the window
and over his rippling muscles and broad chest. He sat
perfectly still, enjoying the momentary respite from the
heat. When it had passed, he reached down into the
saddlebags and fished out a cigar, the bottle of whiskey
and a piece of folded paper. Swinging his feet up onto
the bed, he leaned back against the wall, lit the cigar
then took a pull on the bottle of warm whiskey. Un-
folding the paper, he stared at it as he took another
drink.

It was a wanted poster. The rough drawing of a face
was supposed to be the likeness of one Duke Mc-
Alester. A man wanted for a Wells Fargo stage robbery
and three murders; his latest victim had been a sheriff

in the small town of Haleyville. The reward was one thousand dollars dead or alive. John Law was a bounty man. He had been on the trail of the wanted man and the two confederates who had helped in the robbery, for nearly three weeks now.

Four days ago he had found tracks showing that the three men had split up. J.T. had elected to follow the trail of two riders, which had led him to the town of Killen. Although the poster had only McAlester's face on it, it also carried the descriptions of the two men that had been with him at the robbery and the murders. Using those descriptions, it hadn't taken Law long to find the two men he was after. When confronted in a saloon with the wanted poster, both men had chosen to try their luck against the gunfighter. It had been a fatal mistake for both. Law's reputation as a bounty man was only preceded by his reputation as a gunfighter. Since taking up the bounty trade, John Law had put over twenty men in their graves. The two in Killen had joined that ever growing list.

Before dying on the sawdust floor of that Killen saloon, one of the men had told J.T. that Duke McAlester was supposed to meet up with two cousins in the town of Santa Angela. Law didn't know if he could trust the information, but it didn't seem likely that a dying man would waste his last breath telling a lie. And he didn't really have any choice. A sandstorm that same afternoon had wiped out any chance of backtracking and finding the wanted man's trail. If McAlester didn't show up at Santa Angela, John Law would have to figure the man had broke and high-tailed it for old Mexico. He would give it a few days. If Duke didn't

show, he would head back to Austin, rest up for a week
or so, then set out for someone else. There was no
shortage of wanted men roaming Texas.

Tossing the stub of his cigar out the window, he took
another shot of the whiskey, then leaned back against
the wall and drifted off into a sound sleep.

TWO

★

A SHOT AND the sound of shattering glass brought the gunfighter straight off the bed, his .45 in his hand. It was dark in the room. Night had fallen on Santa Angela and there were rowdy shouts and laughter coming through the window from the street below. Fumbling for matches to light the lamp, Law found it hard to believe that all the hell-raising he now heard was coming from the quiet, dusty town he had ridden into at midday. Putting flame to the wick, he stood next to the window. Holding back the curtain with a finger, he stared down at the street. There were horses tied off everywhere. Drunken cowboys stumbled about, some with bottles in their hands, going from saloon to saloon. Loud piano music came from the saloon directly across the street, while the strumming sounds of a Mexican ballad could be heard coming from the saloon next to the hotel. Apparently, Santa Angela wasn't the sleepy-eyed town it appeared during the daytime.

Rested, his stomach began to growl. He was hungry enough to eat a bear. Shucking his range clothes, he tried to wash the dust and smell of the trail off with what water he had left in the pitcher and the basin. He pulled on a pair of black pants and his last clean white shirt, then slipped on a black vest and his low-crown black hat, strapped on his gun belt and pulled the Colt Peacemaker from its holster and checked the chambers. Having given the cylinder a spin, he dropped the weapon back into place.

Walking toward the door, he paused and, leaning forward, stared into a broken piece of mirror that hung on the wall. His eyes still appeared bloodshot and he could use a shave. The black hair had grown out over his ears. A haircut wouldn't hurt either. The face in the mirror looked older than he remembered, but then he'd been tracking men for more than two weeks; he couldn't expect to look like a Texas gentlemen after that. Rubbing at the stubble, he uttered, "Hell with it." It wasn't like he was having dinner with the Queen of England.

Going out the door, he locked it behind him. At the bottom of the stairs he found the bald clerk awake and standing at the counter. There was a sudden look of surprise on his face. Before he could say anything, J.T. tossed him a twenty-dollar gold piece.

"I'll pick up the change when I leave," he said.

The clerk snatched the gold coin out of the air. He looked at it for a second, then clamped down on it with his teeth. Then he nodded to J.T. and put the money in his pocket.

The café was on the same side of the street as the hotel. As he got closer to the front door, J.T. could smell the aroma of fried meat and beans. It smelled good. He'd been eating his own cooking, such as it was—fried bacon and taters with some jerky thrown in—during the day. He was ready for some real cooking.

J.T. entered and found a table near a window. He looked over the supper crowd. Most were cowboys and vaqueros from the surrounding ranches. A couple of women sat by themselves at a corner table. From the way they were dressed he figured them to be from one of the saloons. They were taking this opportunity to grab something to eat before they went to work applying their trade. It was a job that would last into the early morning hours. One was a big woman with huge breasts that appeared on the verge of popping out of the top of her dress each time she leaned forward. A possibility that didn't go unnoticed by the men sitting around them.

The other woman was just the opposite: short and thin. She didn't look like she would weigh a hundred pounds soaking wet. As far as age went, he couldn't hazard a guess. It had been Law's experience that few women in their line of work ever looked their true age. A girl of seventeen could look to be in her forties after a year of working the whorehouses on the frontier. It was a hard and sometimes dangerous life and one that quickly took its toll on a woman.

A few of the more curious diners cast glances John

Law's way, then went on with their eating. There were a lot of ranches in the area. Cowboys came and went on a regular basis. A strange face in town wasn't uncommon. J.T. noticed a cowhand at the next table cutting into a large steak that covered his entire plate. Next to it was another plate piled with eggs and taters. It looked damn good. That was what he was going to have. Now if he could just get someone to take his order. Where in the hell was the waitress? He was about to call out to the cook when he heard the tap of heels on the board floor and saw her coming toward him. One look at her, and he sat up straight.

She was a tall girl with thick, raven-dark hair, brushed and gleaming. Her skin was olive, an indication of Indian or Mexican blood mixed with white; her eyes were huge, lustrous, and as dark as her hair. Beneath a tight bodice, breasts that were not large or small, but round and firm, jutted outward. The waist was slender, her hips well carved. There was a look of beauty and a certain smartness in her face. When she saw John Law, something kindled in her eyes. They had an impact on each other, as if some unseen force passed between them. Her voice was soft and husky as she stood over him, her pad and pencil in her hand.

"Good evening," she said her eyes meeting his, then dropping away. "May I help you?"

"For now, I'd like some supper," he murmured. Nodding to the next table, he continued, "Same thing that fellow's having would do just fine."

She glanced at the next table and jotted down the order on her pad. She should have left at that point, but she hesitated. Again her eyes met his, but he couldn't read them. He saw the color in her cheeks darken. Suddenly she turned and walked away.

John Law watched her walk toward the kitchen. He leaned back in his chair. Santa Angela, he thought to himself, was going to be an interesting place—in a lot of ways.

Then, as two men walked into the café, he forgot about her, instinctively appraising the new arrivals. The two men stood in the doorway, looking around the room. They were both well dressed in their Sunday goin' to meeting clothes. One wore a gun belt, the other was carrying a shoulder rig. J.T. often wore one himself and quickly recognized the telltale bulge on the left side of the man's coat. The two talked to each other for a minute then made their way across the room to a table near the kitchen and sat down.

The girl came out of the kitchen with his supper. One of the new arrivals slapped the other on the arm and pointed to her as she walked to J.T.'s table. She apparently hadn't noticed the two men when she came out.

She smiled as she set the plates down in front of him and said, "I'll have to bring you a beer. We're out of water, so no coffee either. Will that be all right?"

John T. looked up into her eyes. There was that instant sense of contact again, a mysterious bond of sudden passion and desire. She quickly looked away, as if she were embarrassed at what she was thinking.

He grinned. "Beer will be fine. Thank you."

She turned and headed back to the kitchen. She was halfway across the room before she saw the two men at the table near the kitchen entrance. Her steps faltered and she hesitated for a moment. She glanced back at J.T. with a troubled look. Then, turning, she tried to hurry past them, but the man with the gun belt was loud as he said, "Hello, Rita!"

She neither answered nor bothered to look his way as she passed by.

"Damn it, woman, when I speak to you, answer!" His hand shot out, clamping onto her wrist.

She looked down at him coolly and with a loathing in her voice said, "Let go of me, Harry."

"Not till you soften up some, girl. I'm damn tired of the way you been ignoring me. Just who the hell you think you are?"

She tried to pull away as she raised her hand. "I'll give you somethin' all right—"

"You don't wanta do that, girl." From across the room J.T. saw the man's hand clamp down harder on her arm. Saw her wince in pain. "I've tamed wilder stuff than you, bitch."

With her free hand, Rita slapped the man across the face. The sound of the wicked blow filled the small room.

The man's chair fell over as he sprang to his feet.

"Why you goddamn slut—yer gonna get it now."

Everyone in the café was staring at them. J.T. stood up, his six-foot-two frame crossing the room in long strides.

"Let her go, mister," he said, his voice calm but threatening.

The man jerked his head around, his eyes meeting John Law's.

"I said let her go."

For a long second they stared at one another. Whatever it was the man saw in John Law's eyes was enough to convince him to release the girl. He let his hand drop from her wrist.

"Okay, mister. I let her go, all right?"

Rita shot Law a look of appreciation and quickly disappeared into the kitchen. Harry let out a breath, pulled his chair upright and sat down.

"That wasn't any of your affair, mister," he said. There was still a tight-wound tension in his voice. The bounty man had hurt the man's pride, but he had looked at the gun rig J.T. was carrying and had the good sense to know his own limitations.

Leaning forward and in a quiet tone, so as not to embarrass the man further, he said, "Harry, you don't know me, but if you bother that girl again we're gonna finish this out in the street—you understand?"

Harry nodded, averting his eyes down at the table.

Out of the corner of his eye, J.T. saw the other man easing his hand up inside his coat. As he turned his way, there was no doubting the warning in Law's voice.

"You don't wanta do that, friend."

The man's hand quickly came out from under the coat and went palm down on the tabletop.

"Now, if you two boys are through causin' trouble, my supper's getting cold."

John Law turned his back on the two men and walked back to his table. Harry's friend started to reach for the Colt he carried in the shoulder rig.

"Don't even think about it, Jim."

"What! You gonna let that son of a bitch buffalo you like that?"

Harry's face had lost some its color as he turned to his friend. "Listen, you wanta get yourself killed, that's fine. But leave me out of it. I don't know who that fellow is, but he damn sure ain't no cowhand. You see that rig and the iron he's carryin'—let it be."

Jim shrugged his shoulders and placed his hands back on the table. "Fine with me, partner. Yer the one he made look like an ass in front of these folks, not me."

Harry looked across the room at the big man. "I can get over bein' embarrassed, but you don't get over bein' dead, Jim."

Harry had decided he wasn't hungry after all. As he and Jim left, they glanced John Law's way. The bounty man didn't even bother to look up at them as they passed.

Rita came out of the kitchen with J.T.'s beer. She looked at the empty table to the right of the door. It was plain that she was relieved to see the two men were gone. Placing the beer on the table, she smiled. Her face could light up a room, he thought, as he looked up at her.

"Thank you," she said.

"No need. I don't mind puttin' a loudmouth in his place."

"I am grateful, but I fear I may have brought you trouble. Harry Reeves is not the type of man to forget this."

J.T. set his fork aside and wiped at his mouth with a napkin before he replied, "Oh, I don't know. He backed down pretty fast. Seen men like him before. Their good at pushin' women around, but all mouth and no sand when it comes to standin' up to a man. Don't see much to be worried about there."

Her smiled faded. The pretty face took on a more serious look now.

"It is not Harry, or his cousin Jim Parker, you have to worry about as much as it is the older cousin. He is a very cruel man. Some say he is a gunman for hire and an outlaw as well. He has killed men before."

John Law sat back and draped an arm over the back of his chair. "Oh, is that right?"

"Yes. You must be careful. Harry may have backed down from you tonight, but he will surely tell his outlaw cousin about you. They are expecting him here tomorrow. When Harry tells him what happened, I am afraid the three of them will come looking for you."

"An' just who is this bad man that has you spooked so bad, girl?"

She looked around the room for a second, then leaned forward so others would not hear as she said, "His name is Duke McAlester. He is very good with a gun. He killed two right here in this town only a few months ago. He is a very dangerous man."

She was surprised to see a wide grin cross J.T.'s face. The dying man in Killen had told the truth. All John Law had to do now was wait. This time his prey was going to be coming to him. He saw the concern in her eyes. Reaching out, he took her hand in his and gently squeezed. Her skin was soft. At his touch, it was as if lightning had crossed between them. Her eyes came alive and she was trembling.

"Don't worry about me, Rita. I'm a big boy. I can take care of myself."

He sensed that she already knew that, and that knowledge seemed to excite her even more. She placed her hand over his.

"You appear to be a man that fears little and is accustomed to having what he wants. I don't even know your name."

"Name's John. John Law." He paused, then said, "You're a beautiful woman, Rita. When can you leave here?"

Her cheeks flushed and she took a step back. A look of admiration and shock crossed her pretty face as she stared down at him. "You are J.T. Law—the one they call the bounty man?"

"My friends call me J.T., but other people call me the bounty man. Why?"

"Nothing, *señor*. Its just that . . . that I have heard the name many times before and now . . . here you are in our town. I am just surprised that I would ever meet a man so many talk about here in Santa Angela."

J.T. grinned. "Oh, I'm sure you've heard a lot about me, but don't believe half of it. People have a tendency to stretch the truth on occasion. Does it bother you? My being here I mean?"

"Oh no, *señor*. I am honored that you are here."

"No, it's me that's honored, Rita. I seldom get to talk with a woman as beautiful as you."

She had heard those words before many times, but now, coming from this man, they ignited a fire deep within her that she had not known in a long time. He was a handsome man in a rugged sort of way—the black hair; the deep, blue-green eyes that seemed to peer straight through her. His shoulders were wide and firm, and the narrow waist made him a prize worth any woman's time. Right now she was that woman. It had been a while since she had been with a man—especially a man whose very walk exhibited strength and confidence. A man that others feared.

"Midnight," she said in a husky, almost devilish tone.

The cook interrupted the steamy moment.

"Hey, Rita! Come on, will ya—I got folks waitin' for food here."

She slowly pulled her hand free. "Will I see you at midnight?"

He smiled. "I'll be here at the stroke of twelve. You can count on it."

Leaning forward, she gave him a kiss on the cheek as she whispered, "Thank you, again."

Rita whirled about and headed back to the kitchen, leaving J.T. to finish his supper. As he watched her young, vibrant body disappear through the doorway, he could only imagine what pleasures awaited him at the midnight hour.

Finishing his meal, he left the café and strolled across the street to the sound of the piano music coming from a saloon. It was a noisy, crowded place. Cigarette and cigar smoke hung heavy in the air. Poker games were in progress at most of the tables, while rowdy cowboys with saloon girls on their laps occupied the rest. Two bartenders were busy trying to keep up with the crowd at the bar, which extended from one side of the room to the other.

Men stood shoulder to shoulder, talking and laughing as they drank their beer or poured their drinks from bottles that lined the bar. Intermingled with the crowd of cowboys were more saloon girls, among them the two J.T. had seen at the café. They were wedged between two drovers. One had his hand under the thin girl's dress.

A fight suddenly broke out at the far end of the bar. More drinks were spilled as men scrambled out of the way to give the combatants room. Seeing his chance, J.T. quickly moved through the crowd and found an open spot at the bar. He motioned for a bottle and a glass. A bartender placed them before him then rushed back to the middle of the bar to watch the fight. Pouring himself a drink, J.T. focused his attention on the brawl as well.

The two cowboys involved were both big men. It was clear that no one was feeling brave enough to step in between the two and try to put an end to the fight. That was a sure way for a fellow to get himself hurt.

Heavy blows were dealt back and forth to the cheers of one side or the other. As always was the case, since no one was going to stop the fight, why not take bets on it? Money suddenly began to appear in clenched fists held high in the air, and the men quickly converged on the bet takers. Battered and bloody, the two men continued to battle it out in the middle of the room. The fight finally came to a sudden end when the big man with a beard pinned his opponent against a wall and bit off part of the man's nose. The man screamed he'd had enough as he clasped his hands over his face. Blood was seeping from between his fingers as his friends helped him out the door and toward the doc's office.

The bearded fellow spit out the chunk of meat that had been the end of the loser's nose and raised his arms high in the air to the cheers of his friends. His own face was covered in blood and was already beginning to swell from the pounding he'd taken. But he hardly seemed to notice as his comrades shoved him to the bar and placed a whiskey bottle in his hand. It was his reward for having provided a short but lively round of excitement for the night.

As savage as the fight had been, John Law had seen a lot worse. They occurred almost daily in saloons all over Texas. Life on a cattle ranch was hard work. The average cowboy got a dollar a day and worked from sunup to sundown. At the end of the month, when it was time draw his wages, he was ready to head to town and spend it as fast as he could on women, whiskey and a game of chance. It was his time to howl.

Fights were as common as the wind on those nights. It was only when knives or guns came into play that things could quickly get out of hand and turn deadly in a mere matter of seconds. More than a few honest, hardworking drovers had had a night of fun go wrong. Tempers would flare, a fight would start, and before you knew it, the loser was pulling a gun and someone was dead. Sometimes the cowboy was carted off to jail; other times he could very well end up hanging from a nearby tree before morning, or be gunned down in the street by the dead man's friends. Texas was still a wild and dangerous frontier. Especially where there was little or no law.

Places like Santa Angela were a perfect example.
Because the town was not yet large enough to have a
permanent lawman, the citizens depended on the Texas
Rangers to handle law enforcement matters for them.
The town fell under the jurisdiction of the Ranger company located in San Antonio, two hundred miles away.
Once a month two Rangers would pass through the
town on their way around the circuit. Any murders,
robberies or other serious crimes were reported, and the
details, along with names, if available, and descriptions
were noted. If there were prisoners being held for
crimes, they were handed over to the lawmen at that
time. Few, if any, ever were. The graveyards seemed
to have a considerable number of additions each time
the Rangers came through the small towns like Santa
Angela. It was something the townspeople didn't talk
about, and the Rangers didn't ask.

By ten o'clock, J.T. had had enough of the smoke
and the noise of the saloon and left to get some fresh
air. He still had two hours to wait before Rita would
be finished at the café. Standing on the boardwalk outside the saloon, he saw Harry Reeves and Jim Parker
going into the saloon down the street. For a second he
thought of following, but he changed his mind after
stepping out into the street. McAlester was the man he
was after, not the cousins. The confrontation would
come tomorrow. If Harry and Jim wanted to deal themselves into the game then, so be it. But having seen the
fear in Harry's eyes earlier, J.T. doubted the blowhard
was up to the task of a showdown in the street. Jim
Parker on the other hand had the look of a man that
was willing to take risks. He could be a problem.

Pulling a cigar from his pocket, J.T. lit it and looked up the street. There was a light still burning at the livery. The warm night air felt good as he strolled that way. He was surprised to see the water wagon still setting next to the corral. Walking inside, he found the old man sitting on a bench next to the wall. He was whittling away at a block of wood, a bottle next to his feet. He glanced up as John Law entered.

"Ah, *señor*. You come to see if Pablo has cared for your horse as he promised, no?"

J.T. shook his head. "No, ol' man. I wasn't worried about that. I can tell a man that prides himself on his work and I can see that I wasn't wrong."

The old man had not only watered and fed Toby, but brushed and groomed the mare as well.

"I figured you'd already be on your way to the mountains for more water by now."

As he answered, Pablo motioned for the tall Texan to take a seat on the bench.

"No, *señor*. My wagon, she is still half-full. The people of Santa Angela, they are learning to do with less. But that will be gone by tomorrow night, and I will have to make the trip again." Reaching down by his feet, Pablo picked up the bottle and offered it to J.T. "It is tequila, but I must apologize, I have no glass."

J.T. grinned as he took the bottle. "Who needs one. *Gracias*."

Tipping the bottle back, the sharp bite of the tequila went down hot, nearly bringing a tear to John Law's eye. Passing it back, he nodded, "That stuff's got some kick to it."

Pablo laughed, "*Sí*, my brother in Sonora he makes it special for me."

J.T. wiped his eyes. "You sure he ain't trying to kill you for your business here, Pablo?"

Both men laughed. J.T. pulled two cigars from his vest pocket and offered one to Pablo. He lit it for him, then lit his own and leaned back against the wall. Pablo expressed his surprise that J.T. wasn't in the saloons with the other cowboys and rabble-rousers. J.T. told him about the fight and how after a few drinks he preferred the outdoors and the fresh air. He wasn't much of a drinker—not anymore, but that hadn't always been the case. The old man nodded as if he understood the unsaid meaning of the man's words. The harshness of the land left a man with only two things to do: work and drink. And for many, gringo and Mexican alike, the whiskey had taken over their lives.

The smoked their cigars in silence for a few minutes, then Pablo said, "I would not think a man in your profession would drink much the night before a fight."

This surprised J.T., who raised an eyebrow as he looked over at the old man.

"An' just what profession do you think that would be, Pablo?"

The old man gave a sly grin as he stroked his white goatee with his free hand.

"You did not think one could keep a secret in Santa Angela without being noticed by my people did you, John Thomas Law? My friend Hector was in my stable only an hour ago. He told me you were the famous assassin, John Thomas Law."

"Assassin! Now wait a minute, Pablo," said J.T. There was something about that word that sounded sinister. He'd been called that before and he didn't care for the word. "I wasn't trying to keep any secrets, ol' man. How'd this friend of yours find out who I was?"

Pablo raised his hand. "I am sorry, my friend. The gringos call you a gunman or a shootist. That is simply the word my people use. Hector was in the kitchen at the café when Rita came in all excited and told him who you were. I would think that by now the gringos are the only ones in Santa Angela that do not know you are here."

"Guess that's right. Rita's the only one I've said my name around. Damn."

"Oh, do not fault her, *señor*. She is young and meant no harm."

"Oh, I know. Doesn't really matter. Everyone will know I'm in town tomorrow anyway. Just easier to move around and get a feel for a town when people ain't scared to death of you. You know what I mean?"

The old man nodded, then said, "They say you are the man that killed the Mexican bandit Juan Valdez last year. Is this true?"

J.T. nodded that it was. He had been in pursuit of the murdering Baxter Brothers near Corpus Christi. Valdez and some of his men just happened to be with the Baxters when J.T. caught up with them.

"How do you people know so much about me?" asked John Law.

Pablo raised the bottle and toasted the bounty man.

"I drink to you, John Law. A vaquero that had survived an encounter with you in Corpus Christi came through here one day and told how you had buried Juan Valdez and marked his grave by carving his name and the words 'El Magnifico' into a tree at the head of that grave. As ornery an old bandit as he was, the people loved him. What you did for Juan, few, if any, gringos would have done for a Mexican. That deed has made you almost legendary among my people, John Law."

"That's why Rita looked so surprised when I told her who I was."

The old man laughed. "Oh. I am sure of it. Young women seldom meet a legend. Especially in Santa Angela."

J.T. felt his face go red. "Well now, I wouldn't say I was a legend, but it's a damn sight better than a lot of things I been called."

They both laughed and shared the bottle of tequila again. Setting it beside the bench, Pablo asked, "You are here after someone, no?"

J.T. nodded. "Yeah. But the man I'm after won't be here until tomorrow sometime. Fellow named Duke McAlester. You know him?"

Pablo's face lost its good natured smile.

"*Sí*, I know the man. He is a mean one, my friend. The devil walks with him. He hates my people. Makes fun of them and thinks nothing of killing a Mexican. Says we are no better than Indians, killing either one is not considered a crime by the gringo justice. I am glad you have come for this man. I shall enjoy watching him pay for his crimes against my people. Will you kill him?"

"More than likely. I'll offer him a chance to go back and face a judge, but I doubt he'll take it. Men like him never do. They know there's a rope waitin' for them after the trial and hangin' is a tough way to die. I don't think he'll go peaceful."

The two continued to pass the bottle back and forth as they talked. Their discussions covered everything, from the battle of the Alamo to the War Between The States; Indians, outlaws and lawmen. It was soon clear that both men felt at ease with one another.

At Pablo's insistence, J.T. provided a detailed account of the gun battle in which Juan Valdez had been killed. At the end, J.T. assured the old man that "El Magnifico" had died with the grit and courage befitting a legend of his stature. Pablo in turn related his stories of early day Texas battles with the dreaded Apaches and, later, the Comanches who came to rule the area. It wasn't until the tequila bottle was empty and Pablo started to go for another that John Law realized how late it was. Pulling his gold pocket watch from his vest, he clicked it open and found that it was only a few minutes before midnight. He had been enjoying Pablo's company so much he had almost forgotten about Rita.

Coming to his feet, he placed the watch back in his pocket as he said, "Sorry, Pablo, I've got to be going. I'm supposed to meet someone and I can't be late. I've enjoyed our time together. Thanks for the tequila, my friend."

Pablo nodded and extended his hand as he replied, "I as well. Take care, *amigo*. Perhaps we will talk again before you leave Santa Angela."

"Perhaps. I'll be seein' you before I leave."

Walking down the street, John Law noticed that the town had calmed down considerably compared to earlier. There were fewer horses and drunken cowboys on the street. The saloons were still open, their music beckoning any stray cowpunchers to come on in, the party wasn't over.

As he neared the café, he saw Rita come out the front door and look up the street. Seeing him walking toward her, she smiled and waved. J.T. stepped up onto the boardwalk and placed his big hands on her soft shoulders.

"Told you I'd be here."

She was still smiling that wonderful bright smile as she looked up into the tall man's eyes. "I hoped that you would."

"Where would you like to go?"

The question seem to take the girl by surprise.

"Why, your room, of course."

"You sure?" he asked.

She didn't hesitate with her answer. "Yes, I am sure. That is—if you still want to."

J.T.'s face took on a certain gentleness she had not seen in many men. Taking her arm in his, he walked her to the hotel and went inside. Across the street Jim Parker lit a cigarette as he gave a short laugh and said, "Looks like ya lost your place in the saddle, Harry."

Harry Reeves shot his friend an angry look as he answered, "Yeah, well, every son of a bitch oughta have a little enjoyment before he dies. Duke gets here tomorrow; they'll be plantin' that bastard in the grave-yard 'bout the time I'm climbin' back on that filly—you can count on that."

At that same moment, two hundred miles away in a San Antonio saloon, Frank Neely and Shane Grogan, two highly competent bounty hunters in their own right, were having a drink at the bar when Zack Conway, a friend and saddle partner, rushed into the saloon and up to the bar where the two bountymen were standing.

"Wo there, Zack. What's the rush?" asked Grogan.

A big grin broke across Conway's face. "You boys are gonna get a kick outta this," he said.

Pulling a folded wanted poster from his shirt pocket, the five-foot-five gunman, known primarily for his bushwhacking abilities, opened out the flyer and placed it in front of the two men. The first thing that caught their attention was the amount printed in bold black letters at the top of the poster—$10,000. Unlike other flyers the men were accustomed to, this one didn't have the words "Wanted dead or alive." But rather, simply, "Wanted—Dead!"

As they finished reading the poster, they both looked at one another. With a grin, each raised his glass and they clicked them together as Neely said, "This'll be the biggest one we ever collected, partner."

They downed their drinks and placed the glasses on the bar.

"Let's go," said Neely.

"Right behind ya. Come on, Zack," said Grogan. "Let's ride."

THREE

✦

THE RISING SUN broke through the thin curtains of John Law's room, its warm rays waking him from the first peaceful sleep he'd known in weeks. He felt the weight on his right arm and looked over to see Rita, her raven hair spread over his arm and her pillow. She was sound asleep and as beautiful now as she had been last night. Their lovemaking had been wild and passionate the first time. The second time had been slower, gentle and tender, and was the most memorable time he had ever spent with a woman. Slowly, he tried to slide his arm out from under her head without waking her, but she opened her eyes and smiled up at him. Her soft hand rose and came to rest on his broad chest. Making tiny circles, it moved down to his stomach. Then lower. Any thought of leaving the bed was now gone as he leaned over and took her in his arms again.

There were only a couple of people in the café when J.T. and Rita came in and found a table near the window. They were both famished, and for good reason. They ordered steak and eggs for breakfast. J.T. lit himself a cigar and smiled across the table at her. "You are quite a woman, Rita," he said.

She reached across the table, placed her hand over his and squeezed. "And you are *mucho hombre, mi amor.*"

The waitress brought then coffee. As she walked away, Rita said, "I must admit, I was worried that you would not come back to the café last night. When it came close to midnight and you were not there, I feared I had offended you in some way or perhaps you had gone to a saloon and forgotten about me."

J.T. squeezed her hand back. "Darlin', ain't no man could get drunk enough to forget about you. I had a few drinks and want down to the livery. Nice ol' fellow down there called Pablo. We got to talking and the next thing I knew it was midnight. Hell of an interesting fellow, Pablo."

She grinned a mischievous grin, then replied, "I know—he's my grandfather."

John Law was about to take a sip of his hot coffee when she said that, and he burnt his lips as he looked shocked and bellowed, "What?"

She laughed. "*Sí,* Pablo is my grandfather. He raised me after my parents were killed by Comanches. I was only six when it happened. Even my father could not have done a job better than Grandfather."

J.T. set the hot coffee down and tongued his lips as

he said, "Why, that wily ol' fox never said a word
about that, an' your name come up in our conversation.
He shoulda said something."

"Why? Would it have made a difference?" she
asked.

J.T. thought about it for second, then shook his head.
"No, I guess not."

"Grandfather raised me as a child. He did his job
well, but now I am a woman, I make my own deci-
sions, John T., and last night was a good one—a very
good one."

J.T. was about to say something else when he suddenly stopped and looked out the window as a big man
with a scruffy black beard, a long tan duster, and riding
a chestnut bay passed in front of the window. The man
tied off his horse in front of the saloon next to the hotel
and went inside. Rita leaned forward and looked out.
She caught sight of Duke McAlester as the man was
going through the swinging doors. Sitting back in her
chair, she uttered, "Oh no, its him."

J.T. could feel her hand trembling in his. "It's all
right, Rita. We both knew this was coming. You stay
here. Don't go out in the street. I don't want you to
get hurt."

She started to protest, but he stopped her. "No, Rita.
This is what I do. Now, you stay here, okay?"

Reluctantly she fell silent and nodded, then watched
him walk out the door and across the street. She felt a
cold chill move up her spine. In a few minutes the man
she had made love to only an hour ago could be dead.
She held her breath as she watched this man of courage

and grit check his gun, place it back in his holster and walk inside the saloon.

STEPPING INSIDE THE swinging doors, J.T. saw Parker and Reeves standing at the bar with McAlester. They both looked up as J.T. stepped through the doors.

"That's him!" said Reeves, as he pointed to the doors.

McAlester turned to face Law. Raising his whiskey glass, he downed it, then placed it on the bar without taking his eyes off J.T. He said, "Understand you been givin' my cousins here some trouble, mister. That right?"

J.T. hooked the thumb of his gun hand in his gun belt.

"I don't give a shit about your cousins, McAlester. I'm here for you."

McAlester slowly nodded his head as he asked, "Lawman or bounty hunter?"

"Don't matter much either way, does it? I'm going to give you five minutes. You can come out this door with your belt off and go back for trial, or come out ready to fight. Choice is yours. I'll be waitin' out in the street. Five minutes, McAlester. You don't come out, I'll come back in for you. There won't be any talking then."

Slowly backing out the doors, J.T. walked to the middle of the street and waited.

Inside, McAlester poured them all a drink. Harry's hand was shaking so bad he was spilling half of it on the bar.

"You know that fellow, Duke?" asked Parker.

"Nope. Never seen him before. Don't matter much. There's three of us an' only one of him. Shouldn't be that hard to take him down. I can count on you boys, right?"

Parker pulled his gun and checked the chambers. "Ya damn right ya can, Duke."

Harry didn't answer as quick. Duke looked over at him with hard-set eyes. "Right, Harry?"

"Sure . . . sure you can, Duke." There was no mistaking the fear in Harry's voice.

"Have another drink, Harry," said Duke. "That's why he gave us five minutes. Whiskey can help a scared man screw up the courage to do what he needs to do."

A couple of drinks later, they were ready to go. As they stepped though the doors onto the boardwalk, they found J.T. waiting for them. As the three moved down the steps to the street, Duke whispered, "Spread out before you get set."

The townspeople began to run for cover, seeking a safe place to watch the action. J.T. watched the men as they positioned themselves. Parker was on the far right, Reeves on the left and McAlester in the middle. McAlester wore two Colt .44s in crisscrossed gun belts. Pushing the front of his duster back behind the grips, he set his feet a narrow distance apart—the sign of a man that had found himself in similar situations before.

"You must think you're pretty good with that iron, mister. Takin' on three guns, I'd say you're bitin' off a damn big chew," said McAlester.

"Yeah," said Parker, "what name you want these Mex to put on your tombstone?"

"Law—John Thomas Law," came the reply.

"Oh shit!" uttered Harry Reeves. "J.T. Law—we're dead."

Shane Parker was visibly shaken at hearing the name, but was determined not to back down. He'd told McAlester he would stand by him, and if nothing else, Parker was a man of his word. Duke himself had been caught by surprise when he realized he was facing the most deadly bounty man in Texas, but for him there was no chance to walk away. If he took Law's offer of surrender and a trial, he knew he would be hanging from a scaffold in a month. Better to go down fighting than dancing at the end of a rope.

J.T. gave the men a few seconds to consider who they were up against, then told them, "Reeves, you and Parker don't need to be mixed up in this. I got no warrants for either one of you boys. Stand clear now and you won't get hurt. You got a minute to think on it."

Harry Reeves's face was covered in sweat and his hands were shaking as Duke yelled back, "We're blood, John Law, we stick together."

"Now, wait a minute, Duke," said Reeves in a nervous voice. "Maybe if, if I get ya a good lawyer, ya know, we could maybe get ya outta this. I don't think—"

J.T.'s voice carried the length of the deserted street. "Time's up, boys. What'll it be?"

Harry Reeves unhooked his gun belt and let it fall to the ground as he raised his hands and began to back away.

"You yellow-belly son of a bitch!" yelled Shane Parker. "Ya better hope this bastard kills me, Harry. He don't, I'm goin' to kill you next."

J.T. pushed the tail of his coat back behind the butt of his Colt Peacemaker.

"You call it, boys," he said.

Parker and McAlester glanced at one another then made their move at the same time. As it turned out, Parker was actually the faster of the two. He managed to clear his holster and fire once before the first bullet from Law's .45 tore through his chest, followed by a second that blew the left side of his face away.

McAlester had gone for both .44s at the same time. His draw was fast, but before he leveled the twin 44s, a bullet slammed into his throat. A startled look appeared on the killer's face as he dropped both Colts. His hands went up to his throat. He couldn't get any air. His mouth opened, but only blood came out as he staggered in the middle of the street, trying desperately to suck in air where there was no place for it to go.

Duke McAlester was choking to death. Much the same as a convicted man at a bad hanging. It was a horrible thing to watch. Harry Reeves saw the blood pouring from the man's throat, and turning away, he threw up in the street. In one final desperate act to end this misery, Duke McAlester fell to the ground and reached for one of his guns lying in the dirt. J.T. Law watched with cold calculating eyes as the dying man managed to raise the gun in his bloody hand. As Duke looked up, J.T. thumbed back the hammer on the .45. Once their eyes met, John Law fired. The bullet struck the outlaw in the forehead and blew out the back of Duke McAlester's skull.

The people of Santa Angela began to come out and gather around to stare at the two dead men that lay in pools of their own blood. From the lawyers' office at the end of the street, a short, fat man came pushing his way through the crowd followed by an entourage of other businessmen in suit and ties. The fat man was Ernest Turnbolt, the mayor of Santa Angela, and the others were members of the city council. Pausing to look down at the bloody mess that had once been Duke McAlester, the mayor's face went pale, but he managed to look at J.T. and asked, "Just what was this killin' all about, mister?"

J.T. pulled the wanted poster from his coat pocket and handed it over to the mayor as he said, "Duke McAlester was wanted for murder, dead or alive. Have a warrant for him. That other fellow over there is named Parker, a cousin. He decided to deal himself in on the play. Didn't leave me no choice."

The mayor and the council looked over the poster and quickly discussed the matter among themselves. They all agreed that the killings had been justified and that there was no need for an inquest into the matter. As they passed the poster back to John Law and the crowd was about to break up, someone yelled, "Hey! Here comes the Army."

Everyone turned and watched as the cavalry troop came up to where they were all standing. There were ten black troopers led by a tall, white officer with captain's bars on his coat. Looking down at the dead men, he asked what had happened. The mayor quickly explained the situation and pointed to John Law.

"That's the fellow what done the killing, Captain.

He's a bounty hunter. Name's John Thomas Law. I'm
sure you've heard of him."

The captain nodded that he had. Swinging down out
of the saddle, the officer called for his sergeant, who
quickly dismounted, followed by three other troopers.
He addressed the mayor as he walked up to John Law.

"I've certainly heard of Mr. Law, but never met
him."

Taking a few steps closer, the officer looked the
bounty man in the eyes.

"My name is Captain William Westmore. Temporary
commander of the 10th U.S. Calvary. I see that you
have added a couple more men to your already lengthy
list of dead men, Mr. Law."

"Not by choice, Captain, I can assure you. They
didn't leave me much choice in the matter," replied J.T.

As the heavyset black sergeant and his men came up
alongside the officer, Westmore asked, "Sir, would you
please state your full name for me?"

J.T. gave the man a strange look then said, "John
Thomas Law. What's going on, Captain Westmore?"

The officer suddenly stepped back.

"Take him, Sergeant."

Before J.T. could react, the four soldiers had him in
a firm grip. The sergeant quickly unhooked the bounty
man's gun belt and handed it over to the captain. The
mayor now stepped forward and asked the same question J.T. had asked. "What's going on here, Captain
Westmore? What happened here was a fair fight. We
all saw it. Mr. Law gave those men every opportunity
to surrender but they chose to shoot it out with him. It
was a clear case of self-defense."

Another soldier suddenly appeared carrying a set of manacles and leg irons. In less than a minute he had them locked in place on John Law. Again the mayor started to speak, but the captain cut him off.

"This has nothing to do with what happened here, Mayor. Mr. Law is a wanted man himself."

Removing a piece of folded paper from inside his uniform, the captain opened it out and passed it to Mayor Turnbolt. The little man read it quickly then exclaimed, "Well, I'll be hornswoggled. Says here John Thomas Law is wanted for murder. Even got a ten-thousand-dollar reward on his head." The mayor paused a moment and read the next few lines over a couple of times to make sure he hadn't read them wrong. Looking J.T. in the eye, he continued, "Says here that reward will only be paid if you're—if you're dead, son. Ain't nothing in here about turning you over alive. I'm sorry."

J.T. turned his attention to Westmore. "An' just who is it I'm suppose to have murdered, Captain?"

"Poster says you killed two women outside Fort Worth five or six months ago."

This new revelation caused a mumbling among the crowd as word of the charges was passed among the people for the benefit of those not close enough to hear. They might have been behind J.T. in the killing of McAlester and Parker, but the killing of two women was enough to incite a riot and a hanging in Texas.

Turning to the mayor, the captain asked, "Mr. Turn-bolt, may I have a word with you in private, sir?"

Under the watchful eyes of J.T. and the others, the

two men walked to the corner of an alleyway, out of earshot of anyone.

"Yes, Captain. What is it?"

"Mayor Turnbolt, I don't know if you've thought of it, but this situation could prove to be beneficial to both of us if it's handled right. The Army is tasked with apprehending killers and outlaws whenever the opportunity presents itself; we are, after all, the protectors of the people. However, we cannot accept any reward that may be offered for the men we capture. Page thirty-four section B, paragraph two-point-one of the military handbook forbids government officials from receiving compensation of a financial nature for any reason."

The mayor raised an eyebrow as he said, "Hell, I didn't know that."

"It's a damn stupid regulation," growled Westmore, slapping his riding gloves against his leg in disgust.

"What is it you are proposing, Captain Westmore?"

Regaining his composure, the captain continued, "Rather than taking this man back to Fort Concho and waiting for the Rangers to come for him, which would mean no reward money, I propose to turn Mr. Law over to you and the citizens of Santa Angela. That way you can claim the reward money. All I ask is a modest share of the proceeds—say, three thousand dollars. That leaves you and the town treasurer with seven thousand dollars. If I'm not mistaken, that would be more money than this town has seen in that account since it was founded. We could all benefit from this. What do you say, Mayor?"

Judging from the smile and the look Westmore saw in the little man's eyes, the mayor was already thinking

of ways he could skim off parts of that town money
from the treasury. But the smile quickly faded as Turnbolt remembered the conditions that were required to
claim the reward money.

"But, Captain, the money won't be paid if John Law
is alive. That means someone will have to . . . to kill
him."

The officer's expression never changed as he stated
simply, "Is that a problem?"

Concern was written all over the mayor's face. They
were talking about cold-blooded murder here, and in
front of the whole town at that. It made Turnbolt nervous.

"I just don't know, Captain. I mean, how would it
look to people? You turn this man over to me and in
twenty-four hours he's dead?"

Westmore could see the man didn't have the stomach for this kind of work.

"You have a jail here, right?"

"Sure we do. Ain't nothing fancy, but it serves the
purpose."

"Well, it's simple then, Mayor. You lock John Law
up. Tell people you're going to hold him for the Texas
Rangers. Now, if he tries to escape and just happens
to get shot dead in the process, who could blame you
for that? The guards got a little careless. Law makes
his escape and there just happens to be a couple of men
across the street with rifles who do their civic duty. It's
really quite simple, you see."

The look of concern began to fade quickly as Turnbolt replied, "Yes, I see. Very good, Captain. Can't
have a killer escaping and endangering the good citi-

zens of our town, now can we? Very good indeed."

The two men walked back out into the middle of the crowd.

"Sergeant, give the mayor the keys to those irons. We're turning the prisoner over to the civil authorities," ordered Westmore.

It was clear by the expression on the sergeant's face that he did not agree with the officer's decision. He shot a concerned look in J.T.'s direction. The bounty hunter only smiled. He had watched the two men talking near the alley. This new turn of events didn't surprise him. Ten thousand dollars was a lot of money. J.T. couldn't quote page and number, but he was well aware of the military rule in regards to reward money. He had found it necessary to argue the finer points of that regulation with the Army on more than one occasion. This could only mean the captain had cut a deal with the mayor. The same thought must have crossed the sergeant's mind as well. He started to protest, expressing concern over the well-being of the prisoner and stating he felt John Law would be safer if he were held at the fort.

This brought a stern look from Westmore. "I didn't ask for your damn opinion, Sergeant. Now give Mr. Turnbolt the keys and get mounted. Is that clear?"

The sergeant looked at J.T. as he handed the keys over to the mayor. There was a look of regret in the black soldier's eyes that did not go unnoticed. J.T. nodded his appreciation to the sergeant for his concern and effort. The sergeant quickly turned away.

"All right, you buffalo soldiers, you heard what the captain said, get mounted!"

Westmore turned to J.T. as he pulled on his riding gloves.

"I'm sure you'll find the jail here in town more to your liking than my stockade, Mr. Law. I see no advantage to rewarding discipline problems at the fort by allowing my troublemakers the comfort of a bed, therefore I've had them all removed from the stockade. At least here you will not have to sleep on the floor."

J.T. gave the officer a stern look of his own as he replied, "Too bad you're not as concerned about whether I'm guilty or not."

Walking to his horse, the captain swung up into the saddle and looked down on John Law.

"That's not my job, Mr. Law. I'm sure the Texas Rangers will sort it all out when they come for you. Mr. Mayor, this man is now in your custody. The Army has no further interest in the matter. Good day to you, sir."

The crowd gave ground as the troop wheeled about and headed out of town for Fort Concho. Meanwhile, Turnbolt went among the crowd selecting what he called "special deputies," to guard the prisoner. J.T. saw Rita and Pablo staring at him from the boardwalk outside the café. Pablo had his arm around her shoulders. She appeared to be crying.

The only thing that had gone right so far today was the fact that Duke McAlester was dead. Nothing else had gone as planned. J.T. had figured that after having dealt with McAlester, he might spend a few more days with Rita, but this new trouble had come out of nowhere. As he stood motionless and shackled in the street, J.T. tried to figure out what that poster was talk-

ing about. Who were these women he was supposed to
have killed. When and where? And most of all, why?
There were plenty of questions, for all of which there
were no answers.

The only wanted poster he knew anything about was
one from nearly ten years ago, but that had come after
the war when he was riding with Frank and Jesse
James. And that had been for bank robbery, not murder, and it wasn't even in Texas, but Kansas. None of
this made any sense. One of his best friends was Abe
Covington, a highly respected commander of the Texas
Rangers out of Austin. J.T. had a standing invitation to
stay at the ranch of a Texas senator whenever he
wanted. Hell, he'd even had dinner with the governor
at the state capitol last year. Now here he stood in the
middle of a small town's hot, dusty street, chained like
some mad dog and accused of committing murders that
he knew nothing about.

Having handpicked six of the local men as temporary deputies, Turnbolt had them take John Law to a
small clapboard building that served as the town jail.
It was located at the far end of the street, near the livery
stable. It wasn't much. A single room ten by ten with
a heavy oak door and a small single window to the
front with iron bars.

A big fellow named Red Carver had been deemed
the man in charge of the special deputies. Along with
his tobacco-stained teeth and bad breath he had a dis-
position to match. The fact that Jim Parker had been a
friend of his didn't help. As they opened the door to
the jail, the overpowering smell of urine and pure stink

almost caused J.T. to gag. Carver slammed J.T. in the back and shoved him into the room.

"Now, Mr. Gunman, don't be givin' me no trouble an' I just might see to it ya get something to eat tonight. Had my damn way, we'd string ya up for what ya done to Jim."

J.T. ignored the man as he stood in the middle of the room and surveyed his new surroundings. Red closed the door and slid a heavy bolt in place. From outside J.T. heard Carver telling the men they would keep two of them on duty at all times and would rotate every four hours. Any trouble and they were to fire two shots and the others would come running.

As Carver left, J.T. looked around the room. The only objects in the place were a rickety old bed with a thin, stained mattress and a stinking chamber pot that sat in a far corner. Moving to the window, he looked out. The two guards stood with Winchester rifles, one at each corner of the jail. J.T. had a clear view of the main street and watched as a wagon was brought up and the bodies of McAlester and Parker were laid out in the back then covered with a blanket. The morning's excitement now over, the street was soon deserted as people moved inside to escape another day of what promised to be oppressive heat, the effect of which could already be felt and it wasn't even noon yet.

J.T. turned away from the window and walked to the bed. He was about to sit down when he heard the heavy bolt on the door slide back. When it opened, Turnbolt and one of the guards entered. The guard was carrying a bucket half-full of water. He set it at the end of the bed as the mayor said, "You'll have to ration that water yourself, Mr. Law. As you know, we don't have a lot of it these days. I'll see to it you are provided with some food before sundown. Is there anything else I can do for you?"

The man seemed to be going out of his way to be polite.

"Yeah, you got any idea how long I'll be stuck in here?"

Turnbolt rubbed at his chin with his chubby fingers. "I'd say four—maybe five days at the most before the Rangers come for you. Anything else?"

"Yes. I'd like to have that wanted poster if you still have it on you. Ain't a whole lot of reading material in here."

The mayor reached inside his coat and tossed the flyer on the bed as he laughed. "Ah, a sense of humor. That's good, Mr. Law. A man should try to make the best of things when he finds himself in a situation."

As the mayor turned to leave, he paused at the door and looked back at J.T.

"Mr. Law, I would advise against any thoughts you might entertain about trying to escape. Mr. Carver has instructed his men to shoot to kill if you should attempt anything so foolish. Do you understand?"

J.T. held out his manacled hands and looked down at the short chain and leg irons that restricted his movements. "Don't think I'd get very far anyway, Mayor. But thanks for the warning all the same."

Turnbolt nodded, "Fine, then good day to you, sir."

The two men left. As the bolt was slid into place, J.T. sat down on the bed and opened up the wanted poster. He had seen countless numbers of them over

the last seven years, but there was something about
seeing his own name in bold black letters that twisted
a knot in his stomach. The longer he stared at it, the
more he began to realize that something was different
about this one. Wanted posters issued by the state of
Texas were authorized by the attorney general's office
out of Austin. That authorization and seal were nor-
mally noted at the bottom of every flyer issued. He
scanned the document at the top and bottom, even turning it over to make sure he had not missed it. There
was no authorization to be found anywhere on the paper. This wanted poster had not been sanctioned by the
state of Texas. He began to read the piece of paper that
had suddenly changed his life.

$10,000 DOLLAR REWARD
WANTED FOR MURDER:
JOHN THOMAS LAW

Six foot three inches tall. Above normal build,
black hair, blue-green eyes. Known killer, gunman and bounty hunter. Goes well-heeled. Is
highly proficient with guns and is an all around
dangerous man. Is known to roam areas of
Texas. John T. Law is wanted for the murders
of Mandy Stoval, 17, and Lucinda Ann Croswell, 25 years of age, during a train robbery
March 3rd, 1877, near the city of Fort Worth,
Texas. John Law was identified as a member of
the gang that perpetrated this cold-blooded crime
upon the helpless citizens of Texas and was directly responsible for the deaths of both young
women.

Therefore, issuer has deemed this murder not worthy of a trial for his terrible crime and herefore states that said reward will only be paid to claimant/claimants who can show verifiable proof that the above mentioned assassin, John Thomas Law, is in fact dead.

Claims for this reward must be submitted to Randal L. Dolan, Attorney at Law, Dallas, Texas.

J.T. read and re-read the flyer. His mind was a flurry of activity; a train robbery, two dead women, March 3, 1877. This was mid-August. He tried to remember where he was and what he was doing nearly six months ago. One thing he knew for certain, he wasn't killing people and robbing a train outside Fort Worth, that was damn sure.

J.T. tossed the paper on the bed. This wasn't a wanted poster—it was a ten-thousand-dollar offer to have a man killed. Whoever had took the time to have these flyers printed had made John Thomas Law a marked man. That was a hell of a lot of money, and those looking to collect it could care less if they were after an innocent man or not. Someone had set him up, and it had been done by someone that didn't worry about money. It was a good bet that there were thousands of these posters spread all over Texas by now—that and the fact that there was a high-priced lawyer out of Dallas being kept on a retainer meant big money. But who? And why? The only thing he had to go on right now was this lawyer Randal L. Dolan. If he was going to figure this out, he would have to start with him. But all that didn't matter if he didn't find a way out of this jail and the irons on his hands and legs. That wasn't going to be easy.

Moving off the bed, J.T. began to pace the room. He'd been in rough spots before and always managed to get himself out of a bad fix—and at the moment this was looking like the granddaddy of them all. The sudden turnabout by the Army after the mayor and the captain had their little talk near the alley had convinced J.T. that the two men had hatched some plan to collect the reward money that had been offered on the poster. If that were not the case, he would be sitting in the stockade at Fort Concho right now, not this stink hole of a jail in Santa Angela.

The reward poster was clear about the money. It would only be paid if John Law was dead and that death could be verified. What better witness to that fact than a military commander of a highly respected cavalry unit that was known throughout Texas? Positive identification and the sworn statement to that fact by Captain Westmore would more than likely meet the requirements to satisfy lawyer Randal L. Dolan of Dallas. They were going to have to kill him, but how and when? As J.T. pondered the problem, he finally concluded that it would have to be done sooner rather than later and that whatever they had planned would take place at night. They couldn't just walk in and shoot him dead in the jail, that would raise too many questions, and Turnbolt didn't appear to be the type of man that handled pressure well.

No, the killing would have to take place outside the confines of the jail. An attempted escape was the only logical way to accomplish the plan and remove any doubt people might have. It all made sense: A killer attacks his guards, attempts to escape, is gunned down in the street before he can do harm to the local citizens. Of course, it would be a setup and still be murder, but murder in a way that was acceptable to the good people of the town.

Chained hand and foot, with no gun, knife or other weapons, J.T. knew his chances of getting out of this fix were slim to none at best. Not knowing how or when they would try to set up the escape, he could only wait and see how things played out. Whatever happened, John Thomas Law knew that was going to be his only chance to turn the tables in this game. The waiting was going to be the hardest part.

FOUR

✦

AS THE SUN began to fade and night slowly fell over Santa Angela, Red Carver and the two guards scheduled for the next shift met in Mayor Turnbolt's office. These were all men that Turnbolt knew he could trust to do his bidding for a price and keep their mouths shut afterward. Knowing he would have to deal with first things first, the mayor set a cash box on his desk and removed a handful of money. The two guards would get a hundred dollars a piece, while Red would get three hundred because he was the one that would do the actual killing. These amounts seemed satisfactory to all concerned, and the men quickly got down to how they were going to set up this murder for hire.

They knew they couldn't just open the door and walk away, expecting a man of John Law's experience to fall for such an obvious setup. They had to have a plan, one that would not raise the suspicions of the man they intended to kill. But what? A number of ideas were brought up, but when it got down to the details there were problems with each one. The main one being that no one wanted to include a gun in the breakout. John Law's reputation with a gun was well known; the killings this morning had been a fine example of the man's talent with a gun. But realistically they all knew the man wouldn't try an escape with one. It was Red that finally came up with the answer to their problem. He told them his idea and they all went along. The gun issue settled, they laid out the rest of their plan. In one hour they would be ready to set that plan into motion.

Just after sundown, Rita came to the jail. She carried a basket. It was John Law's supper. The guard stopped her and searched the basket. Taking it from her, he told her she couldn't enter, but was free to talk to the prisoner at the window. While one of the men opened the door and set the basket inside, the other kept a watchful eye on the woman as she stood up on her tiptoes to talk to John Law. J.T. moved to the window and saw the concern in her pretty eyes and the pained expression on her face.

"Hey now, where's that pretty smile I saw on that face this morning?" he said lightheartedly.

Rita tried to smile for him but couldn't do so without showing a hint of fear for his safety. "John, I fear that something bad is about to happen. That bastard of a mayor is a snake. He is not to be trusted, and Harry Reeves is doing all he can to encourage a mob to storm the jail and hang you."

"I know, Rita. I've dealt with their kind before. Don't worry about me. I'll be all right. There is one thing. I hate to ask you this, Rita, but do you think you can get into my room at the hotel, gather up my things and get out without being caught?"

"Of course. Pablo and I both want to do what we can to help you. What do you want me to do with them?"

"Take them to the livery. Have Pablo saddle my horse, pack the gear and keep him out of sight. Can you do that, Rita?"

She stretched as far as she could on her toes and clasped his hand in hers. He could feel the trembling of her body through that hand.

"Yes, my love. What is going to happen, John? You know, don't you? What else can we do? Maybe I can sneak you a gun?"

J.T. gently rubbed the back of her hand. "No, don't try anything like that Rita. It would go bad for you if you were caught. I'm already putting you and Pablo at risk by asking you do these things for me. You just be careful, you hear? If you can't get the things out of the room, don't worry about it."

"Are they going to try and kill you, John?"

"Yes, I believe so. I think your mayor and that Captain Westmore made a deal this morning and I'm the prize. I figure I'll only have one chance to make a break for it, and when I do I'll have to move fast."

One of the guards came over to the window. "Okay, Chiquita. That's it. He's got his supper, now get on outta here 'fore Red catches you an' gives me all kinds of hell."

Rita's hand slid reluctantly from his. She didn't say anything else; she didn't have to—her eyes said it all. J.T. watched her as she made her way down Main Street. As she neared the hotel, she disappeared into an alley. Rita was a resourceful young woman. J.T. knew his gear would be waiting for him if he were fortunate enough to get away.

He looked at his watch. It was just a little before nine o'clock. The next set of guards would be coming on at nine. If they were going to try anything, he figured that would be the crew that would set it all up before midnight. He had to be ready for anything. While he waited, he searched the cell for anything that he could use on the lock of the leg irons, but he found nothing. Frustrated, he sat down on the bed and stared across the room.

His eyes came to rest on the foul-smelling chamber pot in the corner. He had avoided it during his search; now he saw that had been a mistake. "Well, I'll be damned," he uttered to himself as he scrambled off the bed and across the room. Dumping the pot in the corner, he pulled at the carrying handle until he had torn it from the pot. Going back to the bed, he began rubbing one end of the thin metal against his belt buckle until he had worn it down to a size that would fit easily into the lock on the leg irons. Patiently working the tip back and forth and up and down, he became familiar with the inner workings of the lock system. Once he thought he had the small tumblers set where he wanted them, J.T. shoved the metal hard into the hole. The left leg iron clicked and fell free.

A rush of adrenaline brought a spark of hope within

him as he quickly began to manipulate the lock on the right. In less than a minute, it too fell free. He splintered a piece of wood from the bed and placed a small sliver of it into each leg iron so that they would stay in place but he would only have to kick each leg outward to break free when it was time. It had been the leg irons that had worried him the most. He could still do plenty of damage with his hands in irons, but he was going to have to run once this thing started, and with the irons on he would have been lucky to make twenty feet before being shot down in the street. At least now he would have some mobility.

There was some loud talking outside the jail as the new men came on duty. They seemed to be making a point of the fact that Red Carver had ridden out of town and would be back in the morning. J.T. sat on the bed listening to the conversation and laughed to himself. These boys weren't very good at this business. Only a fool would buy the idea that the man in charge of a crew of deputies would go anywhere on the very first night of his new duties. That, and the fact that the men outside were overplaying the out-of-town ploy, only meant that Red was going to be the primary shooter during the escape. Still laughing to himself, J.T. leaned back against the wall. If this was an example of their "Big Plan," he just might have a chance after all.

The move J.T. had been expecting came a little after eleven o'clock. The saloons were still open, but less crowded than the night before. The streets were empty of the regular citizens, who were all safe and comfortable in their beds, and the night was as dark as the ace of spades. Perfect conditions for what they had planned.

One of the guards, a man named Murdock, appeared at the window. "Hey, John Law."

J.T. moved off the bed and shuffled to the window. "Yeah, what do you want?"

The man put on a sympathetic face. "Look here, Law, my name's Rufus Murdock. I think you got dealt a bad hand today. Hell, they should give you a damn medal for killing them two fellows, especially that no-good Duke McAlester. Bastard beat me with a pistol earlier this year. Laid me up for near on to three months. I wanta thank you for that."

"Don't mention it, friend."

"I want you to know, I don't think you did what that there poster says you done. It must be some kind of mistake or somethin'."

"It's plain enough. But I can't do nothin' about it from in here," said J.T.

The man nodded, then said, "Yeah, reckon that's a fact. But look here, I feel like I kinda owe you for what you did to McAlester, and like I said, I think they got the wrong man on that poster. If I get you a gun and help you break out of here, you gotta promise me you won't tell nobody I helped you if you get caught. Damn Red Carver might hang me if he know'd I helped you get away. You gotta promise. What do you say?"

J.T. had to give it to Murdock, the fellow was playing his part to the hilt.

"You got my word, friend."

The man grinned as he replied, "That's good enough for me. I'll be back in a minute."

J.T. watched the man walk away then heard him yell out, "Hey, Charlie, why don't you go get us some coffee? I can handle things here. This fellow ain't goin' no place."

"You sure? Red won't like it just one man on guard here."

"Hell, he ain't even here. Go ahead, it'll be all right."

A few seconds later Murdock was back at the door. The bolt slid back and a hand appeared holding a Colt .45. "Here you go, Law. Now's your chance to make a break for it," said Murdock.

Snatching the man by the shirt, J.T. jerked him inside. Swinging him hard up against the wall, he pulled the Colt from the stunned man's hand and pressed his forearm against Murdock's throat. J.T. stared into the frightened man's eyes. "Where's Red waiting for me?"

Struggling to breathe, Murdock muttered, "Red's gone. He won't be back till mornin'. Why . . . why you doin this to me, Law? I was tryin to help you."

J.T. stepped back, releasing the man. He checked the Colt. To his surprise there was a bullet in each chamber. Either Red was taking a big gamble with the life of one of his deputies, or there was something wrong with the gun. Murdock's eyes were filled with fear as he watched J.T. dump one of the bullets in his hand then smile.

"Seems a little light for a forty-five, friend."

A closer check revealed telltale scratches where the lead and casing came together. They had separated the two, dumped the powder, then replaced the lead. A good plan that would have fooled the average cowboy.

"Where's your rifle, Murdock?" asked J.T. as he

took a threatening step closer to the frightened man.

"It's . . . it's leanin' against the wall next to the door."

"Get it and be careful how you do it."

As J.T. kept a tight grip on the back of the man's shirt, Murdock leaned out the door and brought the Winchester 76 inside. J.T. snatched it from him, shoved the man toward the bed and told him to sit down. Working the lever of the rifle down then back up, J.T. caught the bullet that was extracted in midair. Weighing it in his hand, he smiled over at Murdock.

"You boys didn't think this thing through."

"What're you talking about?" said Murdock.

"You dummied up the loads in the pistol, but you forgot something."

"Yeah, what's that?"

"The Winchester 1876 fires a forty-four-forty. That same ammunition works in the Colt forty-five."

J.T. jacked the rest of the rounds out of the rifle, then emptied out the dummy loads in the pistol and loaded it with the rounds from the rifle. Cocking the hammer back, he walked over to the bed and placed the end of the barrel against Murdock's forehead.

"Now, I'm gonna ask you this just once. Where's Red waiting to bushwhack me when I walk out of here?"

Murdock was shaking all over and on the verge of tears.

"It wasn't my idea. Law. It was the mayor."

"Where goddammit!" demanded J.T., pressing the gun harder against the man's head.

"The woodpile near the livery. Red figured you'd go straight for a horse to get out of town."

"What about Charlie?"

"Across the street. The alley next to the general store. Red figured they'd catch you in a crossfire."

"Get up!" said J.T.

"What're you gonna do? I didn't want no part of this, Law. They made me do it."

J.T. reached into the man's coat pocket and pulled out the hundred dollars he'd been paid. "Yeah, I see how much they made you. Now get over to that door."

Murdock did as he was told. "What're you gonna do?"

"Them boys out there are waitin' for something to shoot at. We wouldn't want to disappoint 'em. Now open the door."

Murdock was shaking and there was a look of desperation in his eyes as he did what he was told.

"Now run for it, you son of a bitch."

Panic clear on his face, Murdock started to protest, but J.T. didn't give him the chance. Pushing him out the door, he fired a bullet at the man's feet. Murdock ran out into the middle of the street screaming for Red not to shoot, but it was too late. Before he could get the words all the way out, Red's rifle cracked. The bullet hit Murdock in the chest and spun him around. Charlie fired next and his bullet struck home, knocking Murdock off his feet. He was dead before he hit the ground. Charlie let out a yell that he'd got him and walked out of the alley. He hadn't taken more than four steps when a voice from the doorway of the jail yelled out, "Hey, Charlie!"

J.T. couldn't see the man's face, but he could imagine the surprise that must have been there when Charlie suddenly realized he was staring down the barrel of a Colt .45 being held by J.T. Law. He tried to bring his rifle up, but it was too late. The .45 flashed in the doorway and roared its thunderous roar. The bullet hit Charlie in the head and the man pitched back into the dirt.

Red was walking toward the jail when he heard the shot and saw Charlie go down. Suddenly John Law was coming out the door and running straight at him. In a panic, Red levered another round into the rifle and fired, but the shot was wild and went wide right. J.T. snapped off a shot. Red felt the burn in his shoulder as the bullet tore a chunk of meat from his left arm. Letting out a yell, the man wheeled about and began running for the livery barn. As Red rounded the corner of the barn, J.T. heard a loud explosion and saw a bright flash of light at the corner. Red's body come flying backward and hit the ground hard. A second later Pablo stepped out of the darkness, a double-barreled shotgun in his hands.

J.T. came up on the body, or what was left of it. He looked at Pablo. Neither man said a word. Rita called out them from the side door of the barn. "Hurry, get inside, both of you."

As they disappeared into the barn, the lights in the houses of the town were coming alive. People from the saloons were already in the street surrounding the bodies of Murdock and Charlie. Harry Reeves began to yell that John Law had broke out and killed both men. "He was runnin' for the barn," shouted someone else.

"Come on, boys!" yelled Reeves, "let's get the murderin' bastard."

With an army of ten men behind him, Reeves headed toward the barn. The men began to spread out as they neared the doors. The mayor showed up and quickly ordered that the killer not be taken alive. They were about to rush the barn when the hoof beats of a horse were heard in the night, coming from behind the barn.

"There he goes!" shouted one of the men as he began to fire at a rider headed off to the east. The others began to fire wildly into the darkness as the sounds of the horse faded in the distance.

"Get saddled, men!" shouted Turnbolt. "There's ten thousand dollars riding away out there. It goes to the man that brings John Law down."

The men nearly knocked each other down scrambling for their horses and saddles. The chase was on, with Harry in the lead.

A MILE OUTSIDE of town, an Army patrol station along the road stopped Pablo and his water wagon.

"What's all the shootin' about, Pablo?" asked one of the soldiers.

"I don't know, my friend. I am going for the water. Maybe too much whiskey. Who knows? What are you doing out here so late?"

"Captain put us out here. Said that fellow Law might have some friends that would try to break him out of jail. Thought that was what all the shootin' was about, but we ain't seen nobody but you all night, Pablo. Probably just a bunch of drunks letting off some steam.

Go ahead, Pablo, I know you got a long way to go."

"Thank you, my friend. Good night."

Pablo snapped the reins and the water wagon rumbled on past the soldiers, headed for the mountain road. It had gone a few more miles when Harry Reeves and his posse rode up on Pablo. They surrounded the wagon as Reeves asked, "Hey, ol' man! You seen any riders out this way tonight?"

Pablo shook his head. "No, *señor*. Only some soldiers on the road back toward town. Why? What has happened?"

Pablo never got an answer, as one of the men said, "Ah, come on, Reeves. The old fool don't know nothin'. We're wastin' time here."

"Yeah, you're right. Let's go."

The riders rode off in the dark, headed back toward the town. Pablo slapped reins to the mules and continued on his way. An hour later he pulled the team off the main road and brought them to a halt in a stand of trees near an arroyo. Climbing up onto the wagon box, he reached over and unlatched the round cover at the top of the wagon.

"We are here, my friend. You can come out now."

J.T. pulled himself up and onto the wagon box. His pants were wet from the water.

"You took a big chance, Pablo. I want to thank you."

"No need. I enjoy the excitement. Reminded me of my younger days. What will you do now?"

J.T. looked around in the darkness. Somewhere out there, Rita was riding his horse. He had heard the shots when she had broke from the barn, and that had worried him ever since they had left with the wagon.

He looked at Pablo. "Do you think Rita is all right?"

The old man smiled. "Do not worry, John Law. My granddaughter knows this country well. She will be here soon. Tell me, why would someone do this thing to you?"

"I wish I knew, Pablo. But you can bet I'm going to find out."

Pablo was about to speak again when both men heard the sound of an approaching horse on the air. J.T. jumped down from the wagon and dashed into the trees. A few minutes later Rita appeared.

"Grandfather, is everything all right?"

"Yes, dear. We fooled them pretty good."

When J.T. came walking out of the trees, Rita climbed down from the horse and ran to him. Throwing her arms around his neck, she pressed herself tight against J.T. and gave him a passionate kiss. They remained that way for some time, until finally the kiss was over.

"Are you all right?" he asked.

"Yes, I'm fine. They shot at me but didn't come close. I could hear them riding around in the night. They are searching for you everywhere. Even the Army is looking for you now. Maybe you should go to Mexico. We have friends down there that could hide you."

"No, Rita. I've got to find out who's behind this business and get it straightened out. Those posters are probably all over Texas by now. I won't run away from something I didn't do."

Rita walked with him to his horse. Reaching up, she removed his gun belt and Colt Peacemaker.

"How'd you get this? I thought the mayor had it in his office."

She smiled that radiant smile of hers. "He did, but his office was near the hotel and I didn't see any lights on, so I sneak in an get it. I figure you will need it."

He gave her another kiss then swung himself up into the saddle. Leaning over, he shook hands with Pablo. "You've both done a lot for me. I won't forget it. I get this thing settled, I'll be back." Looking down at Rita, he concluded, "I promise. Goodbye, my friends."

Rita and Pablo watched John Law ride off into the night, taking their prayers with him.

"Will he be all right, Grandfather?" asked Rita. "Do you think he will really come back here?"

"This is a fighter, my child. He has the courage of a bull; he will not be easily stopped once he has began a quest. Will he come back? Who can say? But by the look in his eyes when he gazes upon you, I would say you have touched this bull's heart. He will come back if he can. I believe that. Now come, we have water to fetch for the people of Santa Angela."

FIVE

✶

FRANK NEELY AND his team of bounty hunters rode into Santa Angela at daybreak. The trio was surprised to see the streets swarming with groups of people at that hour of the morning. As they pulled up at the end of Main Street, Zack called out, "What do you make of this, Frank?"

Neely looked over the small groups of people clustered in the street and along the boardwalks. It was clear from the sense of excitement on the faces of many that something big had happened in the small, out-of-the-way town. Shane Grogan noticed that a number of people kept pointing to a particular spot in the street. As they rode closer, he reined in.

"Frank, look at that," said Grogan, pointing down to two large, rust-colored circles in the dirt. It was blood.

Neely leaned forward, resting his forearm on his saddle horn, and stared at the bloody spots. "I don't know what happened here, boys, but I'd bet my saddle that J.T. Law had somethin' to do with that blood we're lookin' at down there."

They rode a little farther down the street and turned their horses in to the hitch rail in front of the general store, where a group of six men were gathered.

"Looks like you folks had some excitement here. What happened?" asked Neely.

One of the men stepped forward. There was excitement in his voice as he told the story.

"Yes, sure did. Had John T. Law, the gunman and bounty man, locked up in our jail down at the end of the street. He got loose somehow—killed three of our deputies and got clean away. Shot two of 'em down right out there in the street and got the third with a scattergun up near the livery. Got a posse and some troopers from Fort Concho out searchin' for him right now. Got a ten-thousand-dollar bounty on his head, you know. Course, John Law's claimin' he ain't done nothing and the posters are phony, but reckon I would too if I was in his spot."

Neely glanced over at his friends. "Yeah, we know. Thanks, friend. Let's go, boys."

A mile outside of town the group halted. "What do we do now, Frank?" asked Shane. "We got no idea which way Law headed out, and even if we did the trail would be muddled plenty by now."

Neely was silent for a moment as his eyes scanned the countryside. Then he asked, "John Law's got a friend that's a Ranger, don't he?"

Grogan thought about it for a while then replied, "Yeah, a captain of Rangers. Think his name's Covington or somethin' like that. Runs the Ranger outfit in Austin."

"Hell, Frank!" said Zack. "You don't figure a man with that kind of money on his head would go waltzin' into no Ranger headquarters do you?"

Neely set upright in his saddle. "Maybe. Let me see that poster again."

Zack pulled it from inside his shirt and passed it over to their leader.

Frank Neely hadn't really given the flyer much of a look in the saloon, but now, as he studied it closer, he discovered the same things wrong that J.T. had. This wasn't an authorized wanted poster—not by the state of Texas anyway, and he said so.

"What the hell you talkin' about, Frank?" asked Zack.

Neely pointed out the flaws in the flyer to both men.

"So where's that leave us, Frank?" asked Grogan.

Neely folded the poster up and shoved it into his saddlebag. "Don't change a damn thing far as I'm concerned. Poster says ten thousand dollars—dead. State of Texas might not want J.T. Law, but somebody sure as hell does. I don't know why, and for ten thousand dollars I don't really give a damn. You boys in or out?"

The two bounty hunters glanced at one another then nodded to Frank. "We're in."

"I still got the same question, Frank. How we goin' to find John Law?"

"If you suddenly became a wanted man because of

some lyin' wanted posters and you had a friend that was a captain of Rangers in the capital, where would you go?"

Grogan spit, then smiled wide as he replied, "Austin."

"That's right," said Neely. "We don't go chasin' all over the countryside for him. We go to Austin and wait for him to come to us."

"How you know he'll make it that far, Frank? There's gonna be a hell of a lot of people tryin' to claim that reward money between here and Austin."

"He'll make it, Zack" said Neely. "He'll make it because he's J.T. He's been at this game a long time and he's damn good or he wouldn't still be alive."

"You think we can take him, Frank?" asked Grogan.

"I figure by the time he's spent time fightin' and hidin' from them posses and the Army, he'll be pretty worn down by the time he gets to Austin. That should give us the edge we need. I think we can take him with no problem. It's like havin' money in the bank, boys. Now let's go. They got some fine saloons in Austin."

TWENTY MILES TO the southwest, J.T. was down to less than a half-canteen of water and no food. He could see the town of Bracken in the distance, but knew he couldn't risk going in for supplies. No doubt word had spread like a prairie fire of his escape from Santa Angela. Someone in town could recognize him. People would be watching for strangers. Or worse, he would get cornered in the town by a posse or the Army. He had a better chance of outrunning them in the open.

No, he would have to avoid the populated areas in favor of the smaller, isolated, out-of-the-way places, and he knew just the place—Benton's Crossing.

It was just past noon when he saw the broken-down corral of the old trading post come into sight. When it had first come into being, Benton's Crossing had been nothing more than a two-room dugout that served as a whiskey stop for travelers. A few years before the War Between The States, it was purchased by a fellow from south Alabama named Ira Benton. He had expanded on the place and turned it into a first-rate trading post. Guns, clothes, food and blankets—Benton's Crossing had really just begun to prosper when word came of the firing on Fort Sumter.

As J.T. approached the place, he noted the run-down condition of the trading post. The corral was empty and the fences were weathered and broken. A wagon with a busted wheel set next to the main building, which had a roof that was equally in need of repair. As he reined in at the front door, he wondered if Ira Benton still owned the place. Stepping down out of the saddle, he stretched, reached down and loosened the gun in its holster and walked inside. The smell of stale beer and whiskey was a shock to the senses. It took a few seconds for the eyes to adjust to the darkness of the place. As his did, J.T. saw a tall man with salt-and-pepper hair behind the bar blowing dust out of glasses.

As the man turned to see who had come in, J.T. recognized his old friend from the war. Ira looked considerably older than the last time he had seem him, but it was the man from Alabama sure enough. Benton squinted a moment then yelled out, "John T.—is that you? By God it sure as hell is."

Benton come from behind the bar and was across the small room in four long strides. He grabbed Law's hand and slapped his shoulder. "Damn, John T., it's been a long time, partner. Come on in here. How the hell you been?"

"Fine, Ira. I could sure use a drink and somethin' to eat."

Benton called out to his wife, a short little woman of mixed Mexican and Apache blood. She nodded to J.T. as her husband told her to fix some food for their guest. She grunted something in Apache and left the room. Benton pulled J.T. up to the bar and poured them each a large glass of whiskey. J.T. sipped at it as he looked at his old friend. He and Ira had met while in Kansas. Both had been guerrillas during the war. J.T. had been riding with William Quantrill and Ira with Bloody Bill Anderson.

When Bloody Bill had been killed, Benton and some of his men had joined forces with Quantrill. Both men had become close friends with Cole Younger and Frank James. At war's end, Ira had returned to Texas while John T. had remained behind. He participated in the early raids of what later came to be known as the James-Younger Gang. It was those earlier robberies that had put John T. Law on his first and only wanted poster. That had been over ten years ago. J.T. had left the gang soon after that and returned to Texas and the life of a bounty hunter.

"Damn shame about Cole and his brothers," said Ira as he downed the last of his whiskey. "Never have figured out why them boys went that far north to rob a goddamn bank. Minnesota's a god-awful cold place, J.T., let me tell you. Was there once. Never cared to go back neither. And to think Cole and the boys got twenty-five years in a prison up there. Damn shame."

J.T. nodded in agreement as he watched the kitchen doorway for sign of his food. He was so hungry he could feel his stomach rubbing against his backbone. A few minutes later Ira's wife came in with a steak as big as the plate and a side of fried potatoes. Ira talked about the war while J.T. cut his way through the best meal he'd had lately. When he had finished, Ira asked, "So, what are you doin' this far west, J.T.? You got one on the run?"

J.T. almost laughed at the irony of the question. "Yeah, you might say that, Ira. I got to see a lawyer in Fort Worth. On my way there now." Leaning back in his chair, J.T. lit a cigar and watched as Ira poured himself another tall glass of whiskey. It was easy to see why not many things were getting done around the place.

"Tell, me, Ira. How's business?"

Ira downed the whiskey and poured another as he laughed and said, "Hell, there ain't no business no more, John T. You seen the place. Gone to hell. Came back from that war with nothin' and still ain't got nothin'. Folks don't come by here no more. The stages and trains take 'em to the cities and towns with their big stores and fancy shops. Folks don't have no need for tradin' post no more, John T. Not like in the early days. That war hadn't come along, I'd be sittin' pretty now. Business was good before that war, yes sir, damn good. But that's all gone now. Can't bring it back. Now I just set out here watchin' the time pass and thinkin' 'bout what might've been."

John Law could hear the bitterness in his friend's voice. He had heard it before, from others that had returned home to Texas to find that they had not only lost a war, but everything at home as well. It was easy for J.T. to understand, because he had lost everything as well. His mother had died while he was in Kansas and his father not long after that. When J.T. came home, the carpetbaggers and bankers had taken over the family ranch, sold off everything and divided up the land for sale to farmers. He got nothing for his parents' lifetime of work. It had left him a broken and bitter man for that first year. He had turned to the bottle for a while, and after sinking as low as a man could go, he had managed to pull himself up and carry on with his life. He had become a bounty hunter and a good one. Fighting and guns had been all he'd known, and he had turned that knowledge into a profitable enterprise. But now he was the one being hunted.

Ira tried to convince him to stay a few days. They could drink and talk about the old days. J.T. told him he'd like nothing better but that his business with the lawyer couldn't wait. Reluctantly, Ira set about putting together the supplies his friend was going to need for the trip to Fort Worth. By late afternoon, J.T. was outfitted and ready to go. The two old friends were having a farewell drink at the bar when two men rode up. They came inside. Both were well armed and dust-covered, as if they had been riding a long time. They moved to a table and called for a bottle. Ira took one over and returned to the bar.

"Hell, first you, now these two. Most business I've had in two months."

J.T. grinned and raised his glass. "Well, Ira, maybe things are goin' to start goin' your way for a change."

The two friends clinked their glasses together, had a final drink and placed them on the bar. "Well, I gotta be movin', Ira. How much I owe you?" asked J.T.

"Nothin, John T."

Law laughed. "Hell, Ira, no wonder you can't make no money." Pulling the hundred dollars out of his vest pocket that he had taken off Murdock at the jail, J.T. tossed it on the bar. "There you are. That should cover it."

Ira's eyes it up. It had been a long time since he had seen that much money.

"That's too much, J.T. Stuff you got didn't come near to costing this much."

John Law only smiled and turned to walk toward the door. As he did, both men jumped up from the table, their guns drawn.

"Hold it, John Law! Throw up them hands—do it now!"

J.T. did as he was told. They had him covered, and the look in their faces told J.T. they meant business. The taller of the two, a man with a beard and a scar under his right eye, reached forward and pulled J.T.'s gun from its holster. Ira Benton come running out from behind his bar.

"What the hell's goin' on here, you men? What's this about?"

The shorter of the two swung his gun toward Benton. Pulling a poster from his pocket, he tossed it to Benton as he said, "Man's wanted. Now, you stay clear and you won't be gettin' hurt."

Ira picked up the poster and quickly read it. He looked at J.T., the surprise clear in his eyes. This was the first Ira had heard of the wanted poster. He was about the only man in Texas that hadn't heard. "John, is this thing right?"

"No, Ira, it's not what you think. I can ex—" One of the men slapped J.T. across the face with his gun barrel.

"Shut up!" growled the man with the scar under his right eye. "You're caught, John Law. You'll do what we say now."

The other man was laughing and jumping around the room as he shouted, "Goddammit, Charlie, we're gonna be rich! Ten thousand dollars! Yahooo! Rich, I tell you." He suddenly stopped dancing around and looked at his partner. "Let's kill him right now, Charlie. What do you say? That there poster says, 'Wanted Dead'!"

"Hell no!" shouted Benton. "Not in here, boys. I'm the one that'll have to clean up the mess. You gonna do any killin', you do it outside of my place."

Scarface felt the request was reasonable and nodded.

"Okay, Law—outside," he said.

J.T. knew that they would gun him down the minute they were out the door, but there was little he could do about it. Both men had their guns on him and they were keeping their distance, not giving him a chance to make a grab for one of the guns. The tall man led out, then

J.T., with the shorter fellow bringing up the rear.

Just as J.T. ducked down to go through the door, there was a loud roar and a scream as a load of buckshot tore through the last man's back, slamming him into J.T. Scarface turned, and J.T. leaped out the door, grabbing the man's gun hand. The pistol went off, powder burning the back of J.T.'s right hand, but the bullet went into the ground. The two struggled for the gun. J.T. swung a left hook, the fist catching the man above the right cheekbone, stunning him for a moment. J.T. leaned forward and head-butted the man. There was a loud cracking sound. The man screamed as his nose was broken. In a rage, he managed to jerk the gun free for a moment and swung it, the barrel hitting J.T. in the side of the head. Law staggered backward, but not before he kicked the gun from the man's hand. It landed in the dirt a few feet away. With blood pouring from his bloody nose, Scarface dropped to his knees, the pain in his face terrible. He began to crawl for the gun.

"J.T.! Catch!" shouted Benton from inside the dugout.

Law looked back in time to see a sawed-off shotgun come flying out of the darkness of the doorway. He grabbed it in midair, cocked both hammers back and swung the scattergun at Scarface just as the man picked up the pistol and cocked it. The shotgun roared as both barrels let go, the buckshot nearly cutting Scarface in half.

As he wiped a small trickle of blood from the side of his head, J.T. saw Benton come out the door. Tossing the shotgun back to him, Law nodded as he said,

"Thanks, Ira. They had me cold. You sure saved my bacon. I owe you."

"No, you don't, John. I know you'd have done the same for me. You hurt bad?"

"Just a little bummed up. I'll be all right in a few minutes. Get my head cleared up, I'll bury these fellows."

"I'll give you a hand," said Benton.

"No, you done enough, Ira. It's my mess, I'll clean it up."

"Them boys thought they were gonna be rich. Now look at 'em," said Ira.

"Yeah, and it's all for nothing. That poster's a lie. Not even a legal wanted poster. Course, I never could've convinced these boys of that. Too bad."

An hour later, J.T. had finished his work. He had buried both men out back of the trading post. He headed inside. As he entered the room, he found Ira and his wife arguing at the end of the bar. The woman was pointing to something on the bar. His Apache was a little rusty, but J.T. managed to recognize a few words. From what he could make out, she was calling Ira an old fool and a coward. J.T. started to go back outside, embarrassed that he had intruded on the couple. Ira yelled at the woman to get out, then called for J.T. to have a drink with him. As J.T. turned back around, he saw Ira slip the wanted poster under the bar.

The two men had a drink, then Ira helped him with the supplies. They took the saddle off one of the dead men's horses and used the animal as a pack horse. J.T. noticed that Ira seemed nervous, not as relaxed or cheerful as he had been when J.T. first arrived. The supplies loaded, Law agreed to one more drink then he had to go. As they stood at the bar, the two old friends had a final drink. Benton offered up a toast. "To Robert E. Lee and the Confederacy."

"To the Confederacy."

Placing his glass on the bar, J.T. shook hands with Benton and thanked him again for saving his life. As the bounty man turned and walked toward the door, he heard the hammers go back on the sawed-off. Instinct sent him diving to the right just as both barrels erupted, tearing apart the door frame. The Colt .45 was in John Law's hand before he hit the floor. He snapped off two rapid shots, both finding their mark. Ira Benton was knocked back into the row of whiskey bottles, which now tumbled and shattered as they hit the floor. Benton's hand gripped the front of his shirt. There was a stunned look of surprise in his eyes. His wife suddenly appeared out of the back room. Seeing the blood on the front of her husband's shirt and coming from the side of his mouth as he began to sink to the floor, she screamed and ran past Law and out the door.

J.T. had fired without a second thought. Now, as he rose to his feet and glanced at the damage done to the door frame by the double-barreled shotgun, he tried to make sense of it all. Why? Why had a trusted friend that had saved his life only a couple of hours ago now tried to kill him?

Walking behind the bar, he found Ira Benton barely clinging to life. There was blood everywhere. Kneeling down, J.T. looked at him and asked, "Why, Ira? Why?"

Benton's breathing was shallow, and as he tried to talk, blood began to flow down the side of his mouth.

He coughed once, then muttered, "Sorry, John. It wasn't nothin' personal. Things been hard, John. Real hard. Ten thousand—that's a lot of money, John. My old woman got me onto the idea. Just wasn't thinkin' straight, I reckon. Never figured you to be that fast on your feet."

Benton coughed again. Spitting blood, he moaned from the pain, then gripping John Law's hand, he pleaded, "J.T., you won't tell Cole what I done, will you? He'd be real disappointed in me—turnin' on a friend like this. You don't tell him, okay, John? Don't te . . . tell . . . him."

There was one last deep breath, then Benton's hand went limp. He was dead.

John Law carried his friend out back and buried him next to the two men that had died earlier. As he tossed the shovel aside, he stared at the three graves. This was more senseless blood on the hands of whoever had put out that damn poster. Six men were already dead because of it now, and it was clear they wouldn't be the last. J.T. searched for Ira's wife around the area of the trading post, but she was nowhere to be found. Going back inside, he grabbed up four more boxes of ammunition. Pushing them into his saddlebags, he swung up into the saddle. There was an anger building within him like a slow-burning fire. He had been forced to kill a friend because of a lie. When he found the man that had caused this trouble, he was going to remember Ira Benton and vent his anger on that man. Once he had beaten him soundly, he was going to kill him.

SIX

✡

JOHN LAW HAD been gone from the trading post
less than three hours when a troop of Buffalo Soldiers
arrived. They were led by Sergeant Lincoln Towns, the
same man that had objected to J.T. being kept in the
town jail. As they rode up, they saw no signs of life.
Ordering his troops to dismount, Towns told them to
stay on their guard and to search the place. One of them
called the sergeant inside and pointed to the blood at
the door, then led him across the room and pointed out
more blood behind the bar. Towns was about to make
a closer inspection of the mess when another trooper
ran to the doorway and yelled that they had found a
woman half out of her mind behind the dugout. Towns
and the other trooper ran outside and around to the rear.
The woman was sprawled on one of three freshly dug

graves. She was crying hysterically and clawing at the dirt with her hands.

Moving to her side, Towns knelt down and, putting strong arms around her shoulders, pulled her away from the grave. She fought him at first, then realized that the man that held her tight was wearing a uniform. She looked up into his hazel-green eyes and uttered, "He kill my man. He killed him. He killed them all. He is the devil."

"Who killed them, miss? Who?"

"*Muy malo hombre!* Law—John Law."

Towns took her to the front of the dugout and set her down. They gave her some water and he asked what had happened. She suddenly became very calm and told the soldiers that her husband had been at the bar with two customers when John Law had come inside. He had been friends with her husband long ago during the war. She said Law pretended to be friendly, then when they least expected it, he drew his gun and killed all three men. He would have killed her too, but she ran out and hid in the desert until he had gone. Finishing her story, she placed her head in her hands and began to cry again.

Towns stood up and walked a few feet away. As some of the troopers gathered around him, one of them said, "This son of a bitch is a cold-blooded killer, Sarge. We need to shoot to kill when we catch up to him."

Towns shook his head. "I don't believe it."

"What don't you believe, Sarge?"

"That woman's story. I been in Texas a long time now and I heard plenty of stories about this J.T. Law and none of what I heard fits with that woman's story. Besides that, I'm the one put the chains on the man that day in town. I looked him straight in the eyes. You can tell a lot by a man's eyes. I didn't see no cold-blooded killer. He wouldn't have done things like this woman says." Towns paused a moment then turned to one of the troopers. "Davis, take two men and dig up them bodies back there. I wanta see how them men really died. Brown, you come with me."

As the graves detail set about their work, Towns and Brown went back into the dugout. That stopped at the doorway and looked at the shattered wood on the right side. The pattern told the story.

"Shotgun," said Brown. Towns nodded, then walked across the room and stepped behind the bar. His eyes searched the floor for a moment, then he saw what he was looking for. The sawed-off shotgun was on the floor at the far end of the bar, half-hidden under the bottom shelf. Walking through the broken glass and blood that covered the floor, Towns picked up the scattergun and broke it open. He removed both spent shells, then sniffed the barrels. Just as he had figured. It had been fired recently. Next to where he had found the double-barrel, he saw the blood-splattered wanted poster. He picked it up.

Brown was across the room standing at a table near the wall. "Hey, Sarge, look at this."

Carrying the shotgun with him, Towns crossed the room to where Brown was standing.

"Sarge, I'd say there were two people eatin' at this table. You got a bottle of whiskey and two glasses. Two plates, both with beefsteak on 'em and only half ate. For some reason they never finished eatin'."

Towns nodded. "You see any blood around the table?"

"None, Sarge."

Towns and Brown walked back outside.

Davis came walking up to him. "We got 'em dug up, Sarge. Man, a couple of 'em are a real mess."

"Killed with a scattergun, right?"

Davis showed a look of surprise. "Well, yeah, how'd you know that?"

"The woman's husband's the one killed by bullets, right? Say a forty-five, maybe?"

"That's right. Two in the chest. How you know all that? We just dug 'em up." said Davis.

Towns held up the bloody wanted poster and the sawed-off shotgun.

"Ten thousand dollars cuts a lot of old ties. I'd say two of 'em rode in, confronted John Law. The owner an' Law rode for the South during the war. He shotguns one or both of the men to save Law, then starts thinking about the money." Towns walked around the area for a moment then stopped. He knelt down and studied the tracks leading away from the trading post. He then continued.

"The owner helps Law load a horse with supplies." He turned and walked back toward the door. "They go in to have a final drink for old times' sake. Law starts to leave and the owner tries to shotgun him in the back, but he misses and hits that door frame. Law returns fire and kills his friend. He then buries the man. Did you find anything on the marker of the owner?"

"Yeah," said Davis, "this here buckle was stuck to the cross."

Towns took the metal piece and held it up. In the center of the buckle were the initials CSA, for Confederate States of America. Towns felt a moment of sadness sweep over him. Two men that had served as soldiers, had rode together and survived the bloodiest war in the country's history had ended up here, with one trying to kill the other because of money. It was a sad end for any soldier, and even sadder for the one that had survived.

"Sergeant Towns! Dust cloud to the south. Looks like a lot of riders comin' our way," shouted one of the troopers.

"Davis, you and the boys get them fellows back in the ground," said Towns. "Rest of you spread out. Don't know what's comin' our way, but it pays to be ready."

As the riders came closer, Towns recognized the lead man. It was Harry Reeves and his self-appointed posse. They rode right up to the sergeant, covering him in a cloud of dust.

"Just what's going on here, Sergeant?" said Reeves in a demanding voice. "You ain't caught John Law, have you?"

Towns dusted himself off before he answered. "No, but he was here all right. Got three dead men in back to prove it. This wouldn't have happened if we'd held him in the stockade in the first place. We figure he's about three hours ahead of us. We'll have him by morning. You can take your posse on back to Santa Angela. The Army will handle this now."

Reeves wiped the dust from his face and laughed as he turned in the saddle and said, "You hear that, boys? We been chasin' this son of a bitch since he broke jail an' this colored boy here's tellin' us to go home and forget about that ten thousand dollars."

There was grumbling among the posse as Reeves turned back to face Towns. "Now you listen to me, *boy*! Me and my men don't take no orders from niggers, uniforms or no uniforms. We're goin' get J.T. Law, not you Army boys. You got that? We get to him before you do, you better stay clear or there'll be some shootin' for damn sure. You been warned. Come on, boys."

Sergeant Towns and his buffalo soldiers watched the posse ride away.

"Should've killed the whole damn bunch. People more than likely would have blamed it on John Law," said one of the soldiers.

"Yeah," said Towns. "Seems they're blamin him for everything else. Hell, like this mess. Even that damn woman lied about what happened to her husband and those other two bastards. Blamed John Law for murder, when anyone with the sense God gave a jackass can see by the evidence that what happened here was self-defense."

"You don't think he done any what that poster says, do you, Sarge?" said Davis.

"Hell no I don't. Like I said, I saw his eyes when the captain brought out that poster in town. Ain't no way that man had any idea he was wanted for anything. But like Captain Westmore says, I ain't getting' paid to do the thinking. Get mounted. Jefferson, you take the lead. Get on John Law's trail and stay on it. We got to find him before that posse does."

BILLY YOUNG BURST into Captain Covington's office all out of breath. He held a wanted poster in his hand.

"Cap'n, you better have a look at this, sir."

Abe Covington looked up from his desk. There was a stern look on his face as he barked, "Dammit, Billy. What have I told you about bustin' into my office like some wild-ass Indian? Now get back out there and knock like you're s'pose to."

Covington could see the excitement in the young Ranger's face and knew the boy must have some important news. He looked like he was going to explode if he didn't get it out soon.

"But Cap'n this is—"

"Outside, mister!"

Billy jerked his hat off and slapped it against his leg, then turned and raced back out of the room. Standing at the doorway, he balled up his fist and beat hard on the wooden frame. Covington had him do it twice, then yelled, "Get in here!"

Billy stepped in front of the captain's desk and saluted smartly.

"Sir, Ranger Young with information for the captain, sir."

Covington leaned his tall six-foot-three frame back in his chair and lit a cigar before he said, "Report, Ranger."

"Sir, I felt the captain would like to see this as soon as possible."

Billy placed the wanted poster on the desk in front of his commander and stepped back. Covington reached forward and picked it up. When he saw the name on the poster, he rocked forward in his chair. He quickly read the flyer, then looked up at Young, his dark brown eyes staring a hole through the young Ranger. "Where'd you get this piece of shit?"

"Three men at the Ambrose Saloon, sir. They were puttin' together a group to go after that reward money."

Covington jumped to his feet. Running a hand through his long brown hair, he threw on his hat and started for the door. "Come on, Billy."

Billy Young followed his boss from Ranger Headquarters down the street to the capital building. Billy almost had to run to keep up with the long strides taken by the tall man. They took the capital steps three at a time. Once inside, they went straight down the hall to the last office. The sign on the door read, "Jacob Olson, Attorney General." Covington swung the door open, totally ignoring the secretary in the outer office. Before she could say a word, Covington was opening the door to the chief law enforcement officer of Texas. Billy thought of making a remark about knocking first, but thought better of the idea. Abe Covington was not a man you fooled with when he was upset, and right now, Billy Young couldn't remember a time he'd seen his boss this upset.

Olson was sitting at a large round table in the center of the room with five other men in suits and ties. There were papers all over the table—it was obviously an important meeting—but Covington didn't give a damn about that. Walking straight to Olson's chair, the Ranger tossed the wanted poster down in front of the attorney general.

"You wanta explain that, Jake?"

While the other men in the room were stunned and irritated by the crude way Covington had interrupted their meeting, Jacob Olson wasn't in the least bothered by it. He had known Abe Covington a long time and had nothing but the highest respect for the man. He was accustomed to the way the hard-nosed captain of the Rangers operated.

"Wondered when you'd be here, Abe. Just saw one of these myself less than an hour ago. Figured you and John Law being close friends, you'd want to discuss this. Gentlemen, if you would excuse us, the captain and I would like the room for a while. We'll continue with our meeting after lunch. Thank you."

As the other four men departed, Olson asked Billy to close the door and for both of the Rangers to have a seat at the table.

"What's going on, Jake? You know that poster's a bunch of crap, right?" said Abe.

"Of course I do, Abe. If you would have taken a minute to examine it a little closer, you would have seen that this piece of trash was never issued by my office, or the state of Texas for that matter."

Abe grabbed the poster, and his eyes went immediately to the bottom, searching for the standard seal and signature of the Attorney General's Office. It wasn't there.

"I'll be damned—I didn't even notice," he said.

"That's right, you didn't, Abe. If *you* didn't, how many other people that see that thing will? Our friend John Thomas Law has a problem, and it's going to get worse the more people see these things. From what I understand, they're spread all over the state. Whoever it is that wants John Law dead couldn't have come up with a better plan to get the job done. Hell, why send out three or four gunmen to kill him when you can have a whole state do it for you? Ten thousand dollars buys a lot of guns, Abe. He'll have everyone from professional gunmen and bounty hunters to farmers and grandmothers shootin' at him wherever he shows his face."

Abe shook his head. "Could be a lot of people getting killed before we can put a stop to this."

Olson picked up a stack of telegrams and slid them over in front of Abe.

"That's already started. A Captain Westmore at Fort Concho wired my office last night that the town of Santa Angela had been holding John T. when he escaped. They say he killed three local appointed deputies in the process. Those others there are from towns as far away as Sherman, Texas. Two men brought in a body to the sheriff there claiming it was John T. Law and wanting the reward. Of course it wasn't J.T. It turned out to be the sheriff's brother-in-law, who just happened to fit the description. Sheriff there locked them up for murder. Trial will be next week."

"My God," said Abe as he read through the telegrams. In Amarillo, a mob chased a man ten miles, cornered him in some rocks and killed him before they realized it was the wrong man. In San Antonio another man had been killed because he was tall, had black hair and his last name was Lawson. When cornered and asked his name, the mob had only let him get the first part out before they shot him down.

"This has got to stop, Jake. What are you going to do?"

Olson leaned back. "We've sent telegrams to all the law officers in the state to post handwritten notices that the wanted posters are not legitimate. John Law is not wanted and the reward is not valid. I've got the print shop working right now. They'll have a flyer ready by tonight. It's a recall notice. Disclaiming the issue of the wanted poster on John Thomas Law and explaining that that poster is not valid and that J.T. is not wanted for anything. We'll get them out all over the state as soon as we can, but it's going to take time, Abe."

"What about the bastard that started all this with these posters?" asked Covington.

"That's going to be your job, Abe. I'd suggest you start with that lawyer in Fort Worth. If he gives you any of that lawyer-client shit, well, you just do whatever you have to do. But I want to know who's behind this. When you find out, let them know they're going to be charged with murder for every innocent person who dies as a result of this thing. You're going to have to do the hard work, Abe. I can't do anything else until you bring the man responsible to me. Of course, you're authorized to do whatever is necessary to put an end to this. That includes using the military if you think it's needed."

Abe was on his feet. "Well, times wastin', Jake. Thanks. I'll head for Fort Worth on the next train out."

   As the two Rangers opened the door, Olson wished
them luck and asked to be kept informed of their progress. Abe assured him he would be. Back at Ranger
Headquarters, Abe told Billy to get two Rangers and
head for Santa Angela. He wanted a full report on what
happened there. If they should come across J.T., they
were to try and convince him to come back to Austin
where he'd be safe until they got the wanted posters
recalled.
   One hour later, Billy Young and two Rangers were
on their way to Santa Angela. As Abe Covington
boarded a train for Fort Worth, he noticed three men
approaching from the open prairie to the west. Tossing
his bag in the seat, Abe sat down next to it. The train
began to pull out. His attention was still drawn to the
three men that now waited for the train to move out of
their way so they could cross the tracks. There was
something about the three that bothered Covington.
They didn't have the look of everyday cowboys. He
studied their faces as the train passed by, but there was
nothing familiar about them. Still, instinct told him
they could be trouble. Once the train was gone, Frank
Neely and his men crossed the tracks and entered Austin.

SEVEN

✦

IT WAS LATE afternoon when John Law reached the outer edge of the Lipan Flats. The heat hadn't begun to let up yet, hovering just over a hundred degrees. J.T. rubbed at Toby's neck as he watched wavering ribbons of heat rise from the barren flats. Taking a drink from his canteen, J.T. began to have second thoughts about trying to cross the flats in daylight. He might be better off to pull up and wait until after dark. He still had half a canteen and a full rawhide bag of water.

His tired eyes gazed across the flats. There wasn't a tree in sight, only scrub brush and tumbleweed. It would remain the same for the next thirty miles. He could avoid the flats altogether and swing south, go around, then back northeast for Fort Worth. He knew his decision to challenge this terrain had been made

more from anger and a desire for speed than from logic.
The memory of Ira Benton dying in his arms was fu-
eling this impatience. The only thing on his mind was
getting his hands on Lawyer Dolan and twisting a name
out of the man, the name of the man that had brought
all this misery down on not only him, but a number of
innocent people as well.

Toby shook his head and pawed at the ground as if
agreeing with his master that nighttime would be better
for a crossing. Patting the horse's neck, J.T. uttered,
"Okay, girl, we'll find a place to hole up for a while
and get some rest before we cross."

He found a cut-bank arroyo off to the right and led
Toby down into the cut. There wouldn't be a lot of
breeze down there, but hell, there wasn't any air moving anyway, so it didn't make any difference. At least
the cut-bank washout provided some shade for them.
J.T. pulled Toby's saddle off, shucked it up under the
overhang and stretched out against it. To take his mind
off the heat he thought of Rita and Pablo and wondered
how they were doing. He had worried that someone
might link them with his escape. Being Mexican, things
could go bad for them quick if anyone started putting
things together. Shifting his broad shoulders in the sand
and against the saddle, he found a comfortable position
and closed his eyes. John Law couldn't remember the
last time he had been this tired.

THE SOUND OF loud talking and loping horses
brought him out of his sleep. Whoever it was out there
was close. Easing himself up to the rim of the arroyo,

he peeked over the top. It was Harry Reeves and his posse. A man was on the ground brushing sand out of the tracks he'd been following. J.T. could hear some of the men arguing against heading out into the flats, while others tipped back bottles of whiskey and shouted in a drunken state that they'd "follow good ol' Harry as long as the whiskey held out." "Dammit!" whispered J.T. as he scrambled down the slope and quickly threw the saddle onto Toby. In a matter of minutes he was ready to ride. Pulling his Winchester from the saddle boot, he climbed back up to the rim. He saw the tracker walking forward. He suddenly stopped and slowly turned his head in J.T.'s direction. Law couldn't hear what the man said, but he watched the tracker point straight at the arroyo. Reeves and some of the others looked in his direction. They couldn't see him, not yet anyway. Reeves shouted for the men to put the whiskey away, then directed the group toward the arroyo.

J.T. brought the rifle up. He figured they were about a hundred yards out. Levering a round into the chamber, he sighted in on Reeves. He didn't really want to kill any of them, only slow them down, send them scurrying in all directions, giving him time to get out of the cut. They were between him and the flats. He would have to make a break to the southeast. If he could scatter them, he might have a chance to make the low-laying Brady Mountains fifteen miles in the distance.

J.T. moved the sight of the Winchester from Harry Reeves's chest and dropped it a few feet in front of his horse. The rifle jumped and slammed into his shoulder as the first bullet sent sand and dust flying a few feet in front of the horse. The animal reared up, dumping the unsuspecting Reeves on the ground. Four more quick shots had the desired effect. The posse drew their guns and were firing in all directions as they slapped their horses and scrambled left and right, leaving their stunned leader hugging the sand.

Satisfied that he had bought himself some time, J.T. raced down the slope and jumped into the saddle. He ran Toby down the cut until he saw a gradual slope, then brought the fleet-footed animal out of the arroyo and broke into a run for the mountains.

"There he goes!" shouted one of the drunks.

The posse began to fire their pistols as fast as they could, each having visions of collecting the ten thousand dollars for having killed J.T. Law. Of course, none of them had taken the time to realize that their prey was far out of range for their handguns. All that is except one, the tracker. He calmly pulled his long gun from the saddle, eased his horse around and placed the rifle across the saddle. Having flipped up the sight, the veteran scout gauged the distance and slowly squeezed the trigger. The heavy sound of the rifle overshadowed the sounds of the pistols. A cheer went up from the group as they saw John Law slump forward in the saddle and struggle to hang on. He'd been hit.

Reeves leaped to his feet and ran up to the scout. Grabbing the man's shoulder, he cried, "You did it, Tom! Goddamnit, you hit him. Hell of a shot."

Tom Devers pushed Harry's hand away. "Yeah, I hit him. But if he makes those mountains, we'll have a hell of a time rootin' him out of there. Get these bastards rounded up. I ain't waitin' on nobody."

Reeves seemed a little confused. "Hell, Tom, you oughta be jumpin' up and down right now. You coulda got the hit that gets you that reward money."

Devers shoved his rifle back onto his saddle and swung up. He stared down hard at Reeves and the men standing around him.

"You all seem to have forgot one thing—John Thomas Law is a Texan. Ain't nobody here fought no harder for the Southern cause than he did. I don't take no pride in what I just done. None of us should. But what's done is done. Only thing to do now is make sure to end it clean. You comin'?"

The .44-.40 slug from Devers's rifle had entered John Law's lower left back, traveled upward, then glanced off a rib and come out his left side, just below the left nipple of his chest. At the moment of impact, the wind had been knocked out of the bounty man, nearly causing him to pass out. It was all he could do to hang on to the saddle horn as Toby raced toward the Brady mountain range. The distance was now made longer by the burning pain in the man's side. J.T. didn't bother to look back to see if the posse was coming; he knew they had to have seen him take the hit and fall forward in his saddle. If they weren't right behind him, they would be. Like buzzards closing in on a dying prey, they would be picking his bones soon enough.

Through the blinding pain and the pounding of his horse's hooves, J.T. could hear gunfire. It was coming from behind him. The posse was still far behind, but there were those too drunk or too stupid to understand that the man they were after was far out of pistol range. What that did do was make those with the faster horses pull up and swing out to the side in order not to be shot by accident by the idiots.

Two miles to the south, Sergeant Lincoln Towns and his men set their horses on a ridge overlooking the edge of the flats. Towns had his spyglass out. It was focused on the lone rider. He could tell the man was hurt by the way he kept falling forward in his saddle. The man was less than a mile from the base of the Brady Mountains. Moving the glass to his left, Towns focused in on the group of men giving chase. It was Harry Reeves and his posse all right. Towns could see the puffs of smoke coming from the pistols, then a few seconds later hear the report of the gunfire. They were still over a mile behind their prey.

He shoved the telescoping spy glass together and placed it in his saddlebag. Earlier at the trading post he had counted fifteen men in the posse. He had just verified that count again. He looked along the line at his men. There were ten, counting himself. It was decision time for the veteran cavalryman. Reeves and his friends had made it clear that they would not stand for any interference in their pursuit of John Law. Was that bold talk they were willing to back up with action, or just too much liquor? Just as Towns had studied Law's eyes, he had done the same with Harry Reeves and some of his men. What he had seen in those eyes was the same anger and hatred that he had seen since the war between north and south had ended twelve years ago. No cavalry uniform would ever take that look away. He knew if he rode down there now to try and save John Thomas Law, there would be trouble—the shooting kind. The young troopers of his command, none of whom had been old enough to fight in the war, had a good idea what their sergeant was thinking.

"Hell, Sarge, why not let them white folks shoot it out."

The comment drew a stern look from the veteran. "Because that's not our job to just sit on our butts and watch. We're the United States Cavalry, dammit. We're in Texas to protect the rights and lives of the people of Texas. That includes J.T. Law, whether he's guilty or not. Our orders were to apprehend and return the man to Fort Concho. I been in this business since before most of you were born, an' I ain't never failed to carry out an order. I'm not gonna start now. Posse or no posse, we're taking that man back to the fort. We get down there, you watch me close and you follow my lead. If it's a fight them fellows want, then we'll give it to 'em. Understood?"

They all answered that they understood.

"Okay. If there's gonna be shootin', they have to start it. Remember that. Let's go."

HAVING REACHED THE base of the mountains, John T. walked Toby midway up a slope and into a cluster of rocks. He slide off his blood-covered saddle. Pulling the Winchester from its boot, he untied the saddlebags and let them fall to the ground. Every move brought on a wave of pain. His breathing was labored. He figured the bullet had broken some ribs on the left side. He had been shot before, too many times in fact. He was familiar with the pain. But pain could be over-ridden for the moment by a strong sense of survival.

Pulling the saddlebags behind the rocks, he opened
them and removed the boxes of ammunition he had
gotten from the trading post. He also removed the
short-barreled Colt .45 he carried in a shoulder rig and
placed it on a rock next to his Peacemaker. If they were
going to kill him, he was going to make sure he took
as many with him as he could before the end came.

Devers and Reeves were the first two to reach the
base of the mountain. They had watched Law make his
way up the slope as they rode up. Within minutes, the
rest of the men began to join them. Reeves did a quick
count. There were only twelve. He looked back out
onto the flats. He saw the three missing men. One was
drunk and the other two's horses had given out during
the chase. They had left the saddle and were running,
pulling the animals forward by the reins, trying to make
it to cover at the base of the mountain. Devers looked
at Reeves and said, "They'll never make it."

Reeves shouted, "Come on, you men! Hurry up!
Run!"

The other members of the posse began to join in,
yelling for their friends to hurry, encouraging them by
telling them they could make it.

Up in the rocks, J.T. placed the sight of the Winchester on the man still in the saddle. He had no way
of knowing the man was drunk, but it wouldn't have
mattered. He'd tried to warn them off earlier by firing
short and had got shot for his trouble. There wouldn't
be any more warning shots.

The crack of J.T.'s Winchester put an abrupt stop to
the cheering as those already under cover watched the
man on the horse lifted from his saddle and knocked

backward. He hit the ground hard, sending up a cloud of dust around him. He didn't move. They knew he was dead. The two men running suddenly stopped. Looking back at the dead man, they let go of their horses and began to run as fast as they could to cover the fifty yards to the base of the mountain. A second shot slammed into one of the men. He twisted around violently and fell dead. Reeves and the others began to fire wildly up into the rocks, but they had no idea where John Law was firing from. They heard the last man yelling, "Oh God! Oh God!" They were his last words, as a third and final shot blew out the left side of his head. Reeves and the others watched in stunned silence as the man, even with half his head gone, took four more steps before he collapsed in a heap ten yards short of where they were standing.

The shocking sight had left the men of the posse unsure of themselves. No one was firing now. Some men were throwing up. Others ran to their horses, intent on getting away from this place. They had seen enough. Three shots and three dead men. Even ten thousand dollars wasn't worth what they had just witnessed. It wasn't until Tom Devers shouted, "Yeah, you go ahead! Ride on out there in the open and see how far any of you get! Ain't one of you gonna get as far as that dead drunk before that man up there takes you out of your saddle. Go ahead! What are you waitin' for, goddammit! Run! Go On!"

As scared as they were, they knew Devers was right. This wasn't some frightened cowboy or kid that escaped jail that they had trapped up there; this was John Thomas Law, a professional gunman with plenty of nerve, and a damn good shot with a rifle or pistol. He'd just proved that point. Any indecision among the mounted riders was quickly settled when another rifle shot took one of the mounted men's hats off, missing his head only by an inch. The men leaped out of their saddles and crawled to the safety of the rocks.

"Damn, Harry. Just who the hell's got who trapped here?"

Reeves looked to Devers. "Tom, you got more experience at this than any of us. What're we gonna do?"

Devers lit a smoke as he studied the terrain around them. "I warned you we'd be in for it if he made the mountains. You back a wounded animal into a corner, you got to figure he's gonna fight damn hard. We got to spread the men out. Get 'em in positions where they can watch the left and right sides of this mountain. He's halfway up. He can't go no higher without us seein' him and maybe getting a shot at him. We get the men spread out, same'll be true of him movin' to either side. What we got us here is a Mexican standoff. He can't go up or come down, and we can't send anybody out to get around behind him. We could try to move up, but I bet you he'll get three or four of us when we make the move. Man ain't no fool, Reeves. He picked the perfect spot to set up on the side of this mountain."

Panic was starting to set in as Reeves asked, "So what do we do? Wait him out?"

"Can't," said Devers. "We ain't got enough water or food for that. Maybe when it gets dark, we can try movin' up."

"Dark! Hell, we can't wait that long. It's only one man for god sakes. If we spread the men out and all move up at the same time, keep a steady run of lead hittin' all around him, there ain't no way he can cover us all, right?"

Devers set his rifle aside, sat down and leaned back against a rock as he looked at Reeves and replied, "Maybe. You go ahead and do what you think's best, Harry. But I ain't goin' up there till dark."

Reeves's panic had now gone to frustration. It was already over a hundred in the shade, and it was a good seven more hours before sundown. With three men dead and Devers out, that left eleven men. He'd split them into three groups of three and take one man with him up the center. If they all started firing and moving at the same time, they could cover maybe thirty or forty feet at a time. Reload, then move again. Hell, who knows, they might get lucky and get the man with a ricochet. But either way, Harry Reeves was determined to end this thing and end it now.

Calling his men together, he told them his plan. Most were already covered in sweat. They were all hot, tired, hungry and thirsty. All they wanted was to get away from here. But by trapping the man they were after, they had trapped themselves as well. If they wanted out, they were going to have to kill John Thomas Law. To do that, they were going to have to go up the mountain, and they all knew it. Harry Reeves was fair about it; if anyone had a better idea, he was willing hear it. No one did. Reeves broke them down into groups. They would make their first move in ten minutes. Tom Devers again turned down Reeves's offer to join them, but agreed to give them cover fire as they moved up the mountain.

From his fortifications on the side of the mountain, J.T. had a clear view of the area where the posse was holed up. Every now and then he would catch a glimpse of someone moving; a part of a hat or the momentary flash of a shirt or vest, but nothing that was exposed long enough for him to take a shot. But that had all stopped nearly an hour ago. They were up to something, he knew that, but he didn't know exactly what they had in mind. Whatever it was, he was ready.

"Let's go, boys!" shouted Harry, waving his gun toward the mountain.

J.T. heard the yell and brought his rifle up over the top of the rocks, only to be met by some effective rifle fire from Devers, who had selected a good spot of his own. His rifle fire, mixed with the ricocheting lead from eleven other guns, rained a hailstorm of flying lead all around John Law's position. He dropped to the ground and weathered the initial blast. As the firing began to slack off, he came up again with his rifle at the ready. In the blink of an eye he fired a round into the chest of a man on his right, who had forgotten to take cover while he was reloading. Another on the left took a bullet in the shoulder just as he was ducking for cover.

Devers made J.T. pay for those two hits. He fired a rapid series of shots along the edge of the rock next to Law's head. One bullet ricocheted off and sent a shower of dust and rock splinters into the bounty man's face. J.T. dropped his rifle and fought back the urge to scream as the tiny pieces of rock tore into his face. For a moment he was afraid he had been blinded, but he had been lucky, only the dust had gone into his eyes.

He heard Reeves shout another order to move, but he was helpless to do anything about it this time. Reaching up with his left hand, he felt around until his fingers found what he was looking for—a one inch sliver of rock that had been driven into the side of his cheek. Grasping the end of it with his fingertips, he pulled it out of his face.

He couldn't see ten feet. Pulling a canteen to his side, he poured water into his hands and tried to wash the dust from his eyes. He did this twice, and it seemed to help. He did it again. The posse was close enough now that he could hear the smaller rocks rolling down the hillside as the men stumbled on them on their way up. J.T. grabbed the two .45s, cocked the hammers back and fired a series of shots blindly from left to right, hoping to slow them down and let them know he still had plenty of fight left in him.

Gradually his eyesight began to return, but it might be too late. The posse was so close now that he could clearly hear them talking to each other. Reloading the Colts, John Law prepared for the final rush he knew would be coming. Any moment now Reeves and his men would come storming over the rocks firing their guns into him. He didn't know how many there were; at this point it didn't really matter. He was determined to take as many as he could with him, starting with Harry Reeves.

REEVES WAS JUST about to give the order for the final rush when he heard his name called from below. He looked back up the hill to find Tom Devers standing

with his hands raised and surrounded by the troop of
Buffalo Soldiers from Fort Concho. The black sergeant
that he had met at the trading post was calling his
name, telling them to cease their firing and come down
with their hands up. If they did not obey the command,
he was prepared to order his troops to fire on them.
Reeves had thirty seconds to make up his mind. On the
right, Reeves watched as two of his men stood up,
holding their rifles up over their heads, and began to
make their way down the hillside. One of them looked
over at Reeves.

"Sorry, Harry. We ain't fightin' the U.S. Cavalry."

"Dammit!" shouted Reeves. "One more push and
we'd have this bastard. What about the rest of you?
You afraid of those nigger soldiers down there? Or do
you want to let ten thousand dollars slip through your
fingers?"

There were only seven of them left, counting Harry.
The men looked at one another, considering their
choices. "That money's less than forty feet from you
men right now," said Harry, trying to rally support for
one last push forward.

Sergeant Towns repeated his warning. Three more
of the men started to rise to give it up. This sent Reeves
into a rage. Before even he realized it, he'd swung
around and begun firing into the soldiers. Two of them
went down, one dead the other badly wounded. This
action set off an all-out war. The soldiers began to fire
into the seven men of the hill, killing two of the three
that were preparing to give up. Reeves and his men
now began to fire in earnest at the troopers. It had now
become a battle of survival. This was exactly what Lin-

coln Towns didn't want, but Reeves had left him no
choice.

The battle lasted nearly a half hour. In the process
another soldier had been wounded, along with two of
the posse. Out of ammunition, one by one the men of
the posse began to surrender. Sergeant Towns shouted
for them to come down with their hands raised high.
Reluctantly, Harry Reeves stood up and followed the
others down the hillside. The fact that John Law had
not fired a shot since the arrival of the cavalry hadn't
gone unnoticed by Towns. Once they had Reeves in
irons, the sergeant ordered his men up the hill. The men
of the posse watched as the soldiers made the steep
climb, expecting at any minute to see John Law open
fire on them, but nothing happened.

"Maybe we killed the bastard?" said one man.

"Shut up, mister," shouted Towns.

The troopers cautiously moved in on Law's position
from two sides. They disappeared for a moment, then
one of them stepped up onto a rock, placed his hand
on his chest, then slowly brought it out straight and
pointed beyond the mountain.

"What the hell does that mean?" asked Reeves.

Towns halfway smiled as he replied, "That, Mr.
Reeves, means John Law got away. While you was
busy shootin' my men, he slipped out of there and over
the mountain. Looks like you and your men will be the
ones goin' to jail."

Reeves laughed. "A lot you know, boy! Ain't nobody in town going to lock us up for shootin' a couple
of niggers that were interfering in our business."

Towns stepped up to Reeves. His face less than an

inch from the other man's face, his eyes burned a hole
through Harry as he said, "Oh no, boy! You don't get
it. You killed a United States soldier. A cavalryman.
You ain't goin back to no town. You're going to the
stockade at Fort Concho. There won't be no civil trial,
mister. You're gonna get a military trial and a military
judge with Army officers as the jury. To put it plain,
Reeves: We're gonna give you a trial, then we're gonna
put you up against a wall an' use you for target prac-
tice." Towns paused to let all that sink in. Reeves face
turned an ashen gray. "Ain't laughin' now, are you,
asshole? Jefferson. Get this piece of shit outta my
face."

Corporal Jefferson pulled Reeves away and got him
mounted.

"Hey, Sarge. What about John Law?"

The sergeant's sharp eyes searched the ridgeline.
Law was up there somewhere watching them, he could
feel it. But he had a trooper dead and two more
wounded. This would be the first time he'd ever failed
on an assignment, or so his record would read, but he
didn't really see it that way. As far as he was concerned, J.T. Law was an innocent man that had found
himself in an unusual situation. Circumstances had left
him little choice but to take the actions he had to de-
fend himself. An innocent man had escaped. How was
that a failed mission? Raising his hand, Sergeant
Towns gave a salute to the ridgeline and silently
wished the gunfighter good luck.

EIGHT

★

IT WAS LATE in the afternoon when Billy Tyler along with Rangers Tom Overby and Big Mike Fallon rode into the small town of Santa Angela. Their arrival quickly became a source of excitement for the town. Word spread quickly that the men were there to investigate the escape and killings that had taken place in their town. Rumors had already begun to circulate that the mayor and the men killed had somehow planned the escape as an excuse to kill their prisoner. That was a rumor that was sure to interest the Texas Rangers.

As the lawmen made their way to the livery, Mayor Turnbolt stepped back from the window of his office.

"The Rangers are here," he said in a near panic as he turned to face Captain Westmore, who was sitting across the room. "What are we gonna do?"

The captain lit a cigarette. A cocky little smile broke at the corner of his mouth.

"What do you mean—*we*, Mr. Mayor? Wasn't me that made a mess out of this. I had nothing to do with it."

Turnbolt's face went pale as he stammered, "Now, wait a minute, Westmore. This whole damn thing was your idea."

Westmore stood up and laughed. "Oh, is that right? An' I suppose you can prove that, Mayor."

Turnbolt started to say something, but before he could, the captain stepped forward, grabbing the front of the mayor's vest, and pushed him back up against the wall.

"Now, you listen, little man, and you listen good. You even mention my name in this goddamn mess and I swear you'll wish you'd never been born. It was a simple damn plan and you fucked it up—you fix it, and you do it without getting me involved. You got that, you son of a bitch?"

Turnbolt could barely breathe. He quickly nodded his head. Westmore released his grip and walked out the back door. Struggling to get air, the mayor undid his tie and stumbled to his desk. His hands were shaking and sweat poured from his face. He was wishing he had never heard of John Thomas Law.

What was he going to do now? Westmore was not a man to mess with. He had to think. He had been the one that had selected the deputies to watch over the prisoner. He could always say that Red Carver and the others had taken it upon themselves to set up the escape; that the plan had gone wrong and they had got themselves killed in the process. He smiled—that would work. Red never was considered very smart. But just as quickly as he thought he had solved the problem, he realized it had a flaw.

The flaw was the fact that when the bodies had been moved to the undertakers by some of the townspeople, they'd found a hundred dollars in Red's pocket. The man was a known brawler and drunk. He'd never had more than ten dollars on him in his life. Just that morning he had been begging drinks. Now all of a sudden he had a hundred dollars in cold cash. The same was true of the other deputy. A hundred dollars cash. Murdock was the only one that had empty pockets. The find hadn't gone unnoticed by those in the room and had been talked about all over town. Where had these men come up with that much money? Their sudden wealth and the jailbreak that night had raised a number of questions. The local residents found it was suspicious, to say the least.

Turnbolt poured himself a drink and began to pace his office. This whole problem could go away if John Law was killed. But what if he wasn't? What if he came back to town and told how the men had tried to murder him, that he had killed them in self-defense, that someone had put them up to it? Law might come after him too. He was no hero; the gunfighter scared the hell out of him. If he pressed him, he'd have no choice but to involve Captain Westmore. That was no answer. Westmore would have him killed before he ever stepped foot in a courtroom. God, what had he got himself into?

Maybe he could disappear. He had over five thousand dollars in the bank. That would take him far enough away from this place. He could start over, maybe in California or San Francisco. But what about his wife? He'd send her away first, to her sister's in Austin. Once she was gone, he'd draw out their money and disappear for good. The love had gone from their marriage long ago anyway. It had become more of a marriage of convenience than anything else. She'd be all right. Her family had money. They'd take care of her. That was it. He'd simply disappear.

Putting the bottle away, Turnbolt gathered a few personal items from his desk. Taking a final look around, he went out the back door and up the alley, taking the back way to his home. His wife was surprised to see him home so early. He told her that the Rangers were in town and that there could be trouble over the escape and the killings. He didn't want her subjected to that and thought it best she visit family in Austin until this affair was over. It didn't take much to convince her. She had been thinking of taking a trip anyway. The little man breathed a sigh of relief; at least something was going his way. He had her packed and on the six o'clock train that same evening.

Returning home, he started to pack his clothes, then thought better of that. If his clothes were gone, people would know he had left town. Grabbing a couple of shirts and an extra pair of pants, he shoved them into some old saddlebags he hadn't used in years. He would have to get himself a horse. The train was not an option. But what about the money? Once he left, he couldn't return to the bank. He would have to set up a secret meeting with Joe Ballard, the president of the bank. Concoct some story and have him bring the money to him. Next, he had to get out of the house. He had to have a place to hide until he got his money and could slip away. Somewhere no one would expect. A smile broke the worry lines in his face. He knew just the place. Not only was it safe, but it offered a view of the most beautiful breasts he had ever seen, that and a pair of warm loving arms that would hold him and make him forget his troubles, just as they had done countless times over the last year. The two of them had managed to keep their affair secret all this time. No one knew, nor would they ever suspect. The thought of her naked hurried him toward the front door. He closed it behind without looking back. That life was over.

AT THE STABLE, the three Rangers called out for the owner, but no one was around. They unsaddled their horses, tossing the saddles onto the sides of the stables, led their horses in and set the cross bars in place.

"Where you wanta start first, Billy?" asked Overby.

"Well, they don't have a regular sheriff or nothin' here. Guess we'll have to see the mayor first then talk to some of the local folks."

"That is a bad idea, *señor*," said a voice from behind them.

The men turned to see Pablo coming from the back of the livery.

"An' just why is that, mister?" asked Tyler.

"Are you men here to arrest the man they call John Law?"

"No. We understand he already escaped. We're here to find out how a town this size came to have five killin's in less than three days."

"Do you know this John Law?"

"Yes, we know him. Why?" asked Billy.

"You are maybe friends of his?"

"You could say that, I reckon. What are you getting at, ol' man?"

"You are not here for the reward money, then?" asked Pablo, still being cautious.

"Hell, no!" said Big Mike. "There ain't no reward— not a legal one anyway. John Law ain't wanted for nothin'."

Pablo smiled. "I knew I was right about him."

Pablo set down the feed bucket he was carrying and invited the Rangers to sit down on the bench along the wall. "Sit, gentlemen, and I will tell you a story about the excitement that visited our little town the last three days. I think you will find it of great interest."

The three Rangers looked at one another as Billy said, "Okay. Why not? Tell us your story ol' man."

Pablo started from the day J.T. had arrived and told them everything. It was the part about the captain and the mayor that piqued their interest the most. That and the escape. By the time Pablo had finished his story, the Rangers were as convinced as most of the towns-people that the escape had been planned in order to kill John Law. The question of the Army captain's involve-ment in the plan seemed obvious but was going to be a lot harder to prove. Tyler pulled a map from his saddlebags and asked where Pablo and Rita had last seen J.T. Law. Pablo pointed it out on the map. Knowing John Law as he did, Tyler figured the man had headed straight to the only lead he had: Lawyer Dolan in Dallas.

"Now where's this Mayor Turnbolt's office?" asked Billy.

Pablo walked to the doors of the livery and pointed it out to them. "The building this side of the general store. By now I am sure he knows you are here."

Billy thanked Pablo for the information and the three lawmen headed down the street.

Billy banged on the front door but no one answered. He tried the handle, but the door was locked. Big Mike looked through one of the windows. "Ain't nobody in there, Billy."

None of them seemed surprised. "What you want to do, Billy? We could check his house," said Overby.

Tyler looked up and down the street, then replied, "Yeah, we might try that later. Right now what do you boys say we get somethin' to eat at that café Pablo talked about? This fellow Turnbolt don't sound like the kind that would be good at runnin' anyway. We'll find him 'fore the day's over."

"Sounds good to me, Billy," said Big Mike.

"Me too," said Overby. "Give us a chance to check out that gal Rita. We're gonna need a statement from her anyway."

As they prepared to enter the café, Billy said, "We get done eatin' here, might be a good idea to ride out to the fort and see this Captain Westmore."

• • •

AN HOUR BEFORE sundown, Abe Covington arrived
in Dallas. He left the train station and headed straight
for Lawyer Dolan's office. He didn't really expect to
find him there that late, but it was worth a try. When
he arrived at the address, Abe found the office closed.
A check of the merchants still open in the area garnered
him the home address of the lawyer. Realizing the importance of time to J.T., Abe wasted little finding his
way to the Dolan residence. But again his efforts didn't
pan out. A maid answered the door and informed the
Texas Ranger that Mr. and Mrs. Dolan were visiting
relatives in San Antonio and would not be home until
noon the following day.

Frustrated, Abe found a hotel, got himself a room,
then went to bar for a well-deserved drink. He was on
his second whiskey when two men came in and joined
two others at a table almost directly behind where he
was standing. Abe didn't give it much notice until he
heard then talking about John T. Law and the ten-
thousand-dollar reward. He got another drink and lis-
tened as the four men made plans to leave first thing
in the morning. They had heard that John Law was on
the run somewhere around the vicinity of the Brady
Mountains.

One of the men suggested they not waste time and
ride out that night. Another agreed. Abe had heard all
he could stand. Finishing his whiskey, he set the glass
aside and turned around to stare at the four men. It was
a move that made a couple of them nervous. Finally

one of them looked at Abe and asked, "There something bothering you, mister?"

"Nope. My name's Abe Covington. I'm a Texas
Ranger. I just want to make sure I remember each one
of you boys' faces."

"An' just why's that, Ranger? We ain't done
nothin'," said another.

"Not yet, you haven't. But if you collect that reward
on John Thomas Law, I'll be after you boys for murder," said Abe.

There was a surprised look on the faces of the men.
One started to dig out the wanted poster.

Abe stepped closer to the table. "Don't waste your
time showin' me that goddamn flyer on Law either. It
ain't worth the paper it's printed on. Haven't you fellows seen any notices about that damn poster?"

They looked at one another then back to Covington.
"Not a thing, Ranger, an' I got this off the board outside the city marshal's office not two hours ago. You
sayin' it ain't no good?"

Abe's blood began to boil. If Jacob Olson said the
attorney general's office had wired every city and town
about the bogus reward posters, you could take that to
the bank. Jacob Olson was a man of his word. Reaching across the table, Abe snatched the flyer from the
table as he growled, "That's what I'm sayin', cowboy.
John Law ain't guilty of nothin'. It's the man that ordered these posters printed that's in trouble."

"Well, I'll be damned," said one of the men. "I'd
sure hate to be that John Law. Man must have half the
state huntin' him right now."

"Yeah," said another. "Well, hell. There goes our ten

thousand dollars. Looks like another damn winter of ridin' fence, boys."

Abe looked at the man and almost laughed. Leaning on the table, he asked the man, "You know John T. Law, son?"

The young cowboy looked over at Abe. "No, but we heard of him. I figured there's four of us an' only one of him. Seemed like good odds."

Abe straightened up, tossed some money on the bar and set a bottle of whiskey in the center of the table.

"Have a drink on me, boys. You might not think so, but I just saved your lives."

With that, Abe walked out of the saloon and headed for the marshal's office. He found a deputy asleep in his chair, with his feet propped up on a desk. Abe slammed the door behind him. The sound carried like a gunshot in the small room, and the deputy almost fell over backward in his chair as he scrambled to get to his feet.

"What the hell—That wasn't funny, mister."

Abe was across the room in three strides. He tossed the poster on the desk.

"I ain't here to be funny! What do you know about that?"

The man looked at the poster, then back at his unexpected visitor. "Don't know what your problem is, mister, but this here flyer ain't no good. This here fellow, Law, ain't really wanted for nothin'."

Abe stared at the man in shocked disbelief. "Oh— is that right? An' just how do you know that?"

The deputy could hear the irritation in the big man's voice, and he stammered, "Well, 'cause we got this here wire from the capitol." The man shuffled through a stack of paper on the desk. "I know it's here someplace."

"Where's the marshal?" asked Abe.

"Gone to Fort Stockton to pick up a prisoner. Been gone since early this mornin'. Left me in charge. Now if you wanta tell me what this is ab—"

Abe cut the man off. "My name is Abe Covington. Captain of Texas Rangers out of Austin. Now you find that goddamn notice. When you do, you get it to whoever it is that's a printer in this town and you get a hundred more of 'em printed up. Once you done that, you get 'em posted all over Dallas before morning. You got that?"

"Now, wait a minute. You can't come in here like you run the damn place. I—"

Abe took out the letter Olson had given him. He waved it in the man's face.

"You see that. That's from the attorney general's office. I can do damn near anything I want to. Even fire your ass! Now find that wire and do what I told you. I don't see those notices up by morning, you, the marshal, an' anybody else that works for him will be lookin' for new jobs by noon tomorrow."

Abe stormed out of the office, slamming the door behind him so hard that it broke out the window. The deputy stared at the mess on the floor, then began to search through the pile of paper in earnest. Another deputy, who had just completed patrol, walked in. He looked at the broken glass. "Hey, Bob. What happened here?"

"Never you mind. Get yourself over to the printer's

office. Wake his ass up. Tell him I got a printin' job
that has to be done tonight. Tell him to get set up. I'll
be along in a minute."

"Hell, Bob. It's near on to nine o'clock. He ain't
gonna want to—"

"Just do it, dammit! Now, go on."

Back at his hotel room, Abe poured himself a drink
and set down in a chair that faced out onto the main
street. It had taken all the self-control he could muster
not to beat the living daylights out of that deputy. Here
he was sleeping his ass off while somewhere out there
John Law was having to run for his life for something
he didn't do. As he tipped the glass back, Abe wondered how many other places had received Olson's notice and done nothing about it.

Putting a price on a man's head with a wanted poster
was easy; recalling it back was a hell of a lot harder.
Looking up at a bright yellow moon and a sky full of
stars, Abe Covington wondered where the man that had
saved his life nearly nine years ago was right now and
what he was doing. Knowing John Law as he did, he
was certain the man was still alive. He was a survivor.
He was smart, had the reflexes of a mountain cat and
the eyes of an eagle. If anyone could stay alive until
this thing was straightened out, it was J.T. Law.

Finishing his drink, Abe placed the glass on the table
next to the chair and moved over to the bed. He blew
out the lamp and stretched his long frame out on the
overstuffed mattress. He was tired. He needed to get
some sleep. He wanted to be at the Dolan home when
they arrived. The lawyer was going to answer all his
questions, either the easy way or the hard way, it didn't

really matter to Abe which. But he was going to tell Abe who he was working for, that was a fact. A light breeze blew through the curtains and swept over the man that had already fallen sound asleep.

BILLY AND HIS men stopped by the mayor's office again. The door was still locked and there was no one there. The same was true with Rita. The owner said she had left earlier to go see a sick friend and was only supposed to be gone an hour, but had not returned. It had been three hours now. They would have to talk to her later as well. Billy told Overby to find himself a spot where he could watch the mayor's office. The minute he saw anyone there, he was to arrest them and hold them for questioning. He and Big Mike were going to ride over to Fort Concho and see Captain Westmore and get his version of what happened.

As they were about to leave, Pablo mentioned a black sergeant that had been in town that day. He had shown concern for John Law's safety and tried to get the officer to take the man to the stockade. Pablo said he had been ridiculed for his effort. He might be a good man to talk to if he was at the fort. Billy thanked Pablo and told him if he saw Rita to let her know they wanted to talk with her. Pablo told them they could find her at the café. Billy told him what the owner had said. This seemed to surprise Pablo. If Rita said she would only be gone an hour, she would only be gone an hour— not three. He would see if he could find her for them.

It was almost sundown when the Rangers sighted the fort. As they approached the gate, they saw a cloud of dust to the east. A soldier at the top of one of the towers shouted out, "Patrol comin' in!"

As the patrol came closer, Billy saw the lead troopers first, then a group of civilians riding with their hands tied behind their backs. Next came the wounded, and finally the bodies of the trooper and the men killed in the fight.

"Looks like the Army's had a busy day," said Mike.

Billy nodded, as he watched the prisoners led past them and into the fort. He was looking to see if J.T. might be among them. He wasn't. "Let's follow along, Mike. I'm bettin' there's quite a story behind all this."

Sergeant Towns halted the prisoners in front of the commander's office. As he stepped down from his horse, he shouted to Jefferson to take the wounded to the dispensary for treatment. When he turned back around, he saw Captain Westmore coming out of his office. Snapping to attention, he gave his report.

"Sir, Sergeant Towns reporting with fugitive patrol."

Westmore saluted smartly as he stared at the bound civilians before him. "Report, Sergeant!"

"Sir, we pursued the fugitive John Law to Benton's Crossing. There we found evidence that a gun battle had taken place, and the bodies of the owner and two other men. The wife of the owner stated that all three had been killed by John Law."

Sitting their horses off to the side of the headquarters building, Billy and Big Mike glanced at one another at the mention of J.T.'s name.

Towns continued, "We encountered Mr. Reeves and his posse and advised them to go home. That the Army would handle the fugitive's apprehension. The gentleman told us to go to hell and rode away. While approaching the Lipan Flats, we heard gunfire and observed the posse in pursuit of the fugitive, who reached the Brady Mountains and took up a fighting position. As we were en route to their location, the posse made the unwise decision to attempt a frontal assult, which resulted in the death of a number of the members of the group. As you can see, we brought their bodies back."

Westmore looked to the rear of the group and saw the bodies draped over the saddles. It was then that he noticed the body of one of his troopers.

"Sergeant Towns, did John Law kill one of our men?"

"No, sir! Trooper Cole was killed by Mr. Reeves and his posse, sir."

Westmore's eyebrows went up as he barked out, "What did you say?"

"Sir, when we ordered the posse to stop their assault, they replied by firing on the patrol, killing Private Cole and wounding two other troopers. My men had no alternative but to return fire, killing one civilian and wounding two. They finally gave up and I brought them here, sir."

"What about John Law, Sergeant?"

"Sir, during the exchange of gunfire with the posse, the fugitive managed to escape over the mountain. I had wounded troopers and civilians that needed attention. Due to those circumstances, I chose to break off the pursuit and return to the fort, sir."

Westmore nodded. "That's understandable, Sergeant. It was a good decision. Was there any sign that John

Law may have been hurt at any time in all this?'

"Yes, sir. During his flight across the flats for the mountains, one of the posse managed to get off a shot that appeared to hit the man. I saw him rock forward in the saddle, sir, I'm certain he was hit."

"Good work, Sergeant. Have the prisoners placed in the stockade. I will question them one at a time starting in an hour. Of course, I'll need a full written report on this affair. Dismiss the men."

Towns saluted. "Of course, sir. I'll have it on your desk first thing tomorrow."

Billy and Big Mike dismounted. They waited until the sergeant had given his orders and dismissed the troops before they approached him.

"Sergeant Towns," said Billy, "we'd like a minute of your time if you don't mind."

Towns saw the Ranger badges the men were wearing. "Always have time for Texas Rangers. What can I do for you?"

"Understand you tried to help out John Law the day he was arrested by having him placed in Army custody. That right?" asked Tyler.

Towns nodded. "Your information is good. Now we got twelve men dead and four wounded because people didn't want to take that advice. Guess that proves I was right, don't it?"

"I'd say it does that for sure," said Mike.

"I'll tell you somethin' else too. I don't think John Law's done none of them things that poster says either," said Towns.

"You'd be right again, Sergeant. He didn't and he's

not wanted. That poster ain't worth the paper it's printed on."

Towns shook his head. "Goddamn, I knew it. I saw it in his eyes that day. Damn, all these folks dead and for what? Hell, even Law might be dead by now, who knows?"

"We're friends of John Law's, Sergeant. We've been told that your captain might have been involved in a plan to have John Law killed while escaping custody. You know anything about that?" asked Billy.

They could see the question presented a double dilemma for the soldier. Westmore was his commanding officer and he was simply an enlisted man. Westmore was white; he was black. He pondered the Ranger's question for a moment, trying to figure out a way to answer. At that moment, the body of Private Cole was led away. The boy had only been nineteen. Now he was dead and it was all a direct result of Westmore's actions that day in town. Looking Tyler straight in the eye, Towns replied, "You damn right he did. Him and that crooked ass mayor made a deal, no doubt about it. We already had Law in irons. Wasn't no need to turn him over to that town. Hell, they didn't even have a sheriff. There was something funny about that, an' I ain't the only one that thought so."

"Would you be willing to say that in a court, Sergeant Towns?"

"Damn right I would."

"Okay then, we'll take care of that later. For now, we won't let on to the captain what we know until we've finished our investigation. It's John Law that concerns me at the moment. We need to know exactly where it was you last saw him. You say he was hit?"

"That's right. Couldn't tell how bad, but it was a good enough hit to almost take him out of the saddle. I figure he's got to be in a bad way right about now."

Towns spread out his map and pinpointed the exact location where the gun battle had taken place. He then pointed to a cut in the mountain where he thought Law might have escaped during the shooting between the posse and the troopers. Billy's eyes quickly scanned the area and the surrounding terrain.

"How long would it take us to get to that place from here?"

"Three, maybe four hours, but it'll be dark soon. That'll make it a lot harder if you don't know the country out that way," said Towns.

"I'd say you know your way around out there pretty good. You willing to head back out there with us tonight?" asked Billy.

Towns didn't hesitate in his reply. "Let me change horses. This one's plum wore out. Another thing, you'll have to clear it with the captain."

"You get saddled up, Sergeant, I'll take care of that."

Towns headed for the stable while the Rangers entered the commander's office. A soldier in the front office knocked on his door and announced the two lawmen. The captain stood, shook hands with both men, then offered them a chair.

"Thanks, but we ain't got time to sit, Captain. We think we might have a good chance of locating John Law if we leave right away. We think he's wounded and holed up somewhere beyond the Brady Mountains."

Westmore nodded. "Excellent, gentlemen. Please don't let me hold you up."

"Sir, we'd like to take Sergeant Towns with us. He's familiar with the country up that way and could be a big help to us."

They saw a hint of hesitation as the captain leaned back in his chair.

"Oh, I don't know about that. Sergeant Towns is one of my most experienced men. I might need to—"

Billy Tyler wasn't in the mood to put up with a lot of military bullshit, especially when it was coming from a man that he suspected of having tried to kill a friend of his.

"Captain, with all due respect, I don't really need your permission. To be frank, we don't really have time for formalities. The sergeant is leaving with us. If you have a problem with that, I suggest you wire the governor. He has taken a personal interest in this matter. Him and John Law are friends you know. I'm sure he'd be glad to talk it over with you."

The two men turned to leave. When they reached the door, Billy looked back at Westmore. "Oh yeah, one more thing, Captain. If you happen to see the mayor of Santa Angela, would you tell him we have a few questions for him? Thanks."

Westmore watched the men as they mounted in front of his office. Towns rode up and joined them. Walking to the door, the captain watched the three men ride out the main gate. Who would have thought that a gunfighter and bounty hunter was a close friend of the governor? And it was apparent he had a number of friends among the Texas Rangers as well. What had started out as a mere plan to make some quick money had now escalated into a nightmare that could end his military career, if it were discovered that he had been involved in the plot to kill the bounty hunter.

Of course there was no proof of that. The only witness against him for his part in the plot was Turnbolt. That thought sent a chill down Westmore's spine. The man was a sniveling coward that would cave in the minute the Rangers started questioning him. Westmore went back into his office. He pulled a bottle of whiskey from his desk drawer and poured himself a tall glass, all the while cussing himself for having ever got involved in this thing. But hell, who would have figured that a man on a wanted poster with a ten-thousand-dollar reward on his head had such influential friends?

Westmore downed half the glass of whiskey and tried to sort this thing out in his mind. The only link to him was the mayor. He was going to have to rid himself of that albatross around his neck. Turnbolt was going to have to die before those lawmen got their hands on him. But how? People had seen them talking that day. He couldn't do it. If he was seen in town when the mayor turned up dead, the finger of guilt was sure to point his way. No, he couldn't afford to be seen in the town when it happened. He was going to have to get someone else to kill the man for him. But who? Two drinks later it came to him. He shouted for the orderly, who quickly entered the commander's office.

"Yes, sir."

"Orderly. Have the guards at the stockade bring Mr. Reeves to my office."

"Right away, sir."

As he waited, Westmore poured himself another drink and smiled. The worry and concern of only minutes ago were gone. He had the perfect man for the job and it wasn't going to cost him anything. A man facing a military firing squad for the murder of a trooper would surely be willing to trade one killing for another, rather than be put up against a wall. He was betting Harry Reeves was that man.

NINE

✶

THE HOLE IN J.T.'s side hurt like hell. The good news was that it had stopped bleeding. The bad news was that if he climbed back in the saddle it was going to start bleeding again. As much as he hated to stop, he didn't really have any choice. He was already light-headed from the loss of blood and had been on the verge of passing out cold before he reached the remains of what was once Fort Graham. The Army had abandoned the fort some time around 1853. All that remained was a few log and adobe buildings that had caved in on themselves. The wall around the place had fallen and faded away long ago. For the moment it was as good a place as any to lay low until he could get some strength back. The bullet he'd taken had passed clear through his body, but he had lost a lot of blood. Rest was the best medicine for the time being.

WHEN HE WOKE from a short nap he was hurting, hungry, thirsty and tired. To add to his troubles, a ricochet from the posse or the soldiers had killed his pack horse. He had managed to grab the water bag and a handful of jerky while the men below were fighting each other, then leading Toby by the reins, he had used the distraction to escape through a cut in the mountain. Once he heard the shooting stop, he had expected to see the Army troopers coming over the hill after him, but they never appeared. He was grateful for that. It had saved him from having to make the decision whether to fire on them or give himself up.

Leaning back against one of the old adobe walls, J.T. realized he was going to have to change his plans. There was no way he could reach Dallas in his present condition. He thought about it and decided to head southeast. If he could reach Ranger Headquarters in Austin, he could get help from his old friend Abe Covington. The challenge would be getting there without getting killed. On his way to Fort Graham he had had to dodge three separate groups of well-armed men that were searching the countryside for him. Luck had been on his side. If any one of them had picked up on his trail, it wouldn't have been much of a gunfight. In his present condition J.T. was easy prey for the hunters. His only hope was that he could stay clear of them until he was able to ride again.

He chewed on a piece of jerky as he stared up at the
stars. He still hadn't been able to put this whole business together. Nothing made any sense. J.T. had tried
to form a list of enemies in his mind, but soon gave
up on that idea when he realized how long the list
would be. Bounty hunters and gunfighters had few
friends and plenty of enemies. He was going to need
help to find the person behind this, and Abe was the
one friend he knew he could depend on. Easing himself
away from the wall, J.T. laid his head back on his
saddle, closed his eyes and drifted off to sleep.

He awoke to the sounds of voices off in the distance
to the north. It was just after sunrise. A sudden move
for his rifle sent a shock wave of pain through his side,
reminding him that he had been shot. As painful as the
wound was, he didn't have time to worry about it now.
The voices were coming closer. So close that he could
make out what they were saying.

"Hey! Over here. I got some tracks leadin' to the
south."

J.T. couldn't see them yet, but he could follow their
movements by the small clouds of dust raised by their
horses as they zigzagged back and forth beyond the
dunes. It was only a matter of time before they crested
the dune and would be headed his way. Levering a
round into his Winchester, the bounty man placed his
Colts on the ground beside him. He wasn't going to be
locked up in a cage again. They'd have to kill him.

The first man to appear at the top of the dunes was
a vaquero. He wore a large sombrero. As he halted his
horse, he brought up a rifle and placed the butt on his
leg while he scanned the ruins of the old Army post.

A second man soon joined him. This was an American riding an Appaloosa. The two men talked for a moment. The vaquero pointed toward the ruins of the building J.T. was hiding in, then to two more farther over to the left. The winds overnight had wiped away any trace of J.T.'s movement into the ruins. The men weren't sure if he was there or not, but they weren't taking any chances. Unlike Reeves and his posse of amateurs, who had rode blindly into the sights of J.T.'s rifle, these men were obviously professionals, men accustomed to hunting other men, J.T.'s brothers in trade—bounty hunters.

J.T. watched as the two men turned and disappeared back behind the dunes. The dust clouds would now be the only clue he would have as to what they were going to do. There was nothing for a few minutes, then he saw a cloud rise off to the left, then another rise slowly to the right. The dust would give him a clue as to which direction they were moving, but couldn't tell him how many he was facing—not that it really mattered. He couldn't run; he was going to have to fight—it didn't matter if it were two or twenty. The only thing he had going for him was the element of surprise. They weren't really sure if he was there. That would give him the edge. He would get the first series of shots. He had to make them count. For the next ten minutes there was nothing—no sound, no dust clouds, nothing; only an uneasy silence.

The first group appeared from the left. There were five of them. The vaquero and three more came riding in from the right. J.T. could pick and choose his targets, but he waited. The center was the weak spot in his defenses. The American with the Appaloosa wasn't with either of the two groups; that could only mean he would be coming up the center. J.T. had guessed right. Within seconds the Appaloosa and four others rode over the top of the dune and straight for John Law. He leveled the rifle and fired, knocking the first man out of the saddle; three more rapid shots and two more men went down. Before he could get a shot at the other two, he had to duck for cover as gunfire from the left and right began to hit around him like rain.

Men were shouting to each other, each group wanting the other to move in, but neither wanting to be the first to face the deadly accurate fire they knew John Law capable of. Slowly, working from building to building, they began closing in on the wounded man. The closer they came, the more costly the price. One man hesitated, then stuck his head up only to have it blown apart. Another ran for the cover of an adobe wall but was too slow; J.T. put two bullets into him before he made it ten feet. Bullets were hitting all around John Law, but somehow he managed to avoid being hit. His clothes were not fairing as well. His left foot went numb as a bullet tore the heel from his boot. Two bullets ripped through his right pants leg, while another tore a piece of his collar from his shirt.

They were pressing him now. He didn't have time to reload the Winchester. The roar of the .45s quickly replaced the sharp crack of the rifle. Although the weapons had changed, J.T.'s accuracy hadn't. The rider on the Appaloosa came charging straight for the adobe wall J.T. was hiding behind. The big horse leaped, clearing the wall. The rider found himself staring down into the eyes of the man he sought to kill. In that flicker of a second their eyes met. They both fired at the same time. John Law felt the hot lead from the man's .45 burn its way along the side of his neck, and saw the man's hat fly off.

At first he thought he had missed his target. The Appaloosa wheeled about, the rider still in the saddle. His gun arm hung limp at his side, but he still held the Colt in his hand. He was staring down at J.T., but there was no expression in his face and the eyes had a distant look about them. J.T. pulled the trigger to put another shot into him, but there was only a click as the hammer fell on a spent cartridge. J.T. had fired all six shots. His gun was empty. The Appaloosa slowly walked toward him as J.T. grabbed for his other gun. He knew he didn't have a chance. The gringo had him and John Law knew it. Even as he grabbed for the gun, he expected to feel a bullet any second. But it never came. As the horse stopped only a few feet from him. J.T. looked up and saw the hole under the man's chin. The jump hadn't taken the man's hat off his head; a bullet had gone in under his chin and blown the back of the man's head out. The man's death grip on the saddle horn was all that was keeping him in the saddle. A ricochet spooked the Appaloosa and she reared up, dumping the dead man at J.T.'s feet.

Reaching out, J.T. pried the gun from the man's hand as he said, "I'll be joinin' you soon, friend."

All the activity had opened the wound in J.T.'s side again. He reloaded his guns and prepared himself for the final rush which he knew would be coming anytime now. He didn't have to wait long. The bounty hunters rose up and charged forward from both directions at the same time. As J.T. started to fire, he suddenly saw three of the men coming from the right cut down by a hail of bullets and tumble into the sand. Seconds later he saw dust fly from the shirts of two men on the left as they were hit and fell dead.

J.T. took down two more as the stunned attackers paused to search out who had fired on them from the dunes. All the attackers from the right were dead. J.T. watched the survivors on the left scramble back toward their horses. He started to fire on them, then lowered his gun. They had had enough. They were running away; that was all that mattered now. There had been enough killing for one morning. Whoever it was that had joined the fight must have felt the same. They allowed the men to mount and ride away.

J.T. slumped back against the wall, a gun in each hand. He was still alive thanks to someone. His sigh of relief was short lived. What if his saviors were no more than another group of reward seekers that had simply eliminated their competition? He cocked back the hammers on both guns. This fight may not be over yet. Pushing himself up so he could see over the wall, he scanned the dunes. There was no sign of anyone. He began to feel himself slipping down the wall. The loss of blood and the excitement of the fight had drained every ounce of strength from him. His vision became blurred and he was beginning to feel light-headed. The will to fight was still as strong as ever, but the body no longer could. He struggled to focus and to keep his eyes open. He could feel himself slipping away. He heard voices coming toward him. He tried to raise his guns, but they now seemed so heavy. He tried to fight off the darkness that was closing in around him but it was hopeless. He fell sideways, felt his head hit the sand, then there was nothing, only the darkness.

J.T.! COME ON, J.T., wake up." The words seemed to be coming from a long ways off, but the voice sounded familiar.

"Come on, J.T. You're too damn mean to die. Open those eyes."

The words were clear now. He struggled to lift his eyelids. Felt a wet rag being wiped over his face. The water felt good. Slowly he began to open his eyes. The figure he saw in front of him was still a blur, but with each wiping of the rag it came more into focus. It was a young face. A face he'd seen before. J.T. shook his head from side to side to try and clear it. Another voice, this one deeper, said, "He's startin' to come around now."

The face before him became clear now. It was Billy Tyler. The young Ranger from Abe Covington's Ranger company in Austin. But where had he come from and what the hell was he doing out here in the middle of nowhere?

Raising a hand, J.T. rubbed at his eyes to make sure he was seeing what he thought he was, then he asked, "Billy . . . Billy Tyler?"

"That's right, John T. We almost got here too late. Can you sit up?"

"Hell, I thought I was sittin' up. Give me a hand."

There was some laughter and John Law realized there were other people there besides Billy. Once he was sitting upright, he saw another familiar face kneeling behind Tyler. It was Sergeant Towns. Next to him was another man, a big fellow. J.T. didn't recognize the man but saw the Ranger badge on his vest.

"What the hell are you boys doin' out here?" asked J.T.

"Savin' your ass," said the big man with a laugh. "Them fellows had you pretty well boxed—they was comin' in for the kill when we got here."

"You're right about that. But how'd you know where I was?"

"Sergeant Towns here figured after you got out of them mountains there was only a couple of places a wounded man could go. He led us here. Like Big Mike said, we hadn't got here when we did, them fellows would've had you slung over a saddle for damn sure," said Tyler.

J.T. looked past Tyler and at the smiling sergeant. "Guess I owe you, Sergeant. You ain't carryin' no leg irons with you this time, are you?"

Towns shook his head. "No, sir. Not this time. From what these Rangers tell me, we was wrong to put 'em on you to start with. I'm sorry about that."

J.T. shook his head. "That's all right, Sergeant. I'd say you more than made up for that, thanks."

Billy leaned forward and lifted the edge of the bandage they had placed around Law's waist. "You got a fair size hole there, J.T. Did a little pokin' around while you was passed out; best I can tell it went clean through. Bleedin's stopped too. Think you can ride?"

J.T. looked up at the young man. "I take it Abe's already heard about the wanted posters and the jail-break at Santa Angela. Some fellows got themselves killed there."

Tyler nodded. "We know all about it, J.T. Captain's already left for Dallas to see that lawyer fellow, Dolan. We know the posters are a lie, but he figured there'd be some questions that'd have to be answered about three men being killed during your escape. He sent me, Overby and Big Mike here to get the straight of what happened."

J.T. looked the boy in the eyes. "It was a damn setup from the start, Billy. Just didn't turn out like they planned."

"That's what we kinda figured," said Mike. "Sergeant Towns here, and a fellow named Pablo back at the livery, told us pretty much the same thing."

As they were helping J.T. to his feet, he asked, "Did you see Turnbolt yet? He's the mayor. Him and that army captain from the fort were the ones that set it up."

"No, we haven't found him yet, J.T., but don't worry, we will. Overby's still in town watchin' his office. He's got orders to arrest him soon as he shows himself," said Billy.

Once they had J.T. in the saddle, the others mounted. Big Mike looked around at the dead men scattered among the ruins. "What about them fellows?" he asked.

J.T. spit, then replied, "Coyotes gotta eat too, Mike.

Them boys grabbed for the golden ring and missed. Can't do nothin' for 'em now."

Tyler wheeled his mount around. "He's got a point, Mike. Let's go. We should be able to make Santa Angela by sundown."

TEN

★

ABE COVINGTON WAS waiting for Lawyer Dolan when he and his wife stepped off the train in Dallas. Abe approached them and introduced himself. Tipping his hat to the lady, he asked if he might have a word with her husband alone. Dolan, a tall, wiry man with a mustache and glasses, started to protest, but there was something about the look in the big man's eyes that told him that would be a bad idea. Excusing themselves, the two men walked to the end of the platform. Dolan was clearly agitated by this unexpected interruption.

"All right, Captain Covington. Since you have already delayed me from going to the comfort of my home after a rather long trip, what is it that you want?"

The Ranger pulled the wanted poster from inside his

coat pocket and opened it out. "I want the name of the man who hired you for this."

Dolan recognized the poster at once. It had been nothing but trouble since he had taken on the job. That was one of the reasons he had left town.

"I'm sorry, Captain, but I can't give you that information. My client preferred to remain anonymous. I'm sorry."

Abe took a step closer. He was almost in Dolan's face.

"You're gonna be more than sorry if you don't give me that name, mister."

Dolan tried to move, but his back was against the wall of the depot office. "Now see here. You can't intimidate me like this. Information between a client and his lawyer is private. You're a peace officer; you know that."

"Well, let me tell you somethin' you don't know, Mr. Dolan. The man's name that you have on this wanted poster ain't wanted for nothin'. He didn't have anything to do with no train robbery. You get what I'm sayin', Mr. Lawyer? You're offerin' ten thousand dollars for someone to kill an innocent man."

Dolan's eyes became dazed and he began to stutter. "But, that's . . . that's not possible. I was told, told that this man was one of the robbers and the one that killed those two girls. There has to be some mistake."

"You're damn right there is. Hell, this isn't even recognized as a legal wanted poster in the state of Texas. This ain't no more than an offer to commit a murder. Now who are you workin' for, Dolan? I want a goddamn name an' I want it now!"

"Randal, are you going to be much longer, dear?"

Abe turned to find the man's wife walking toward them. He whispered to Dolan, "Tell her we have to go to your office."

The lawyer's hands were shaking and he was turning a little pale, but he did as he was told, telling his wife he would be home in an hour. They watched her leave in a carriage, then walked to Dolan's office. Inside he went to the safe, opened it and removed some documents. Placing them on the desk in front of the Ranger, he said, "I can't tell you who paid me, but if I were busy and you happened to find the file and read it without my knowledge, what can I say?"

Dolan turned his back and crossed the room where he busied himself with other papers, leaving Abe at the desk alone with the file. Abe opened it and began to read. The first few pages were filled with fancy lawyer talk like "herefore" and "hereby known as." He didn't give a damn about that; all he wanted was a name. He found it at the bottom of the third page—Warren Gentry.

"Dolan! Who is this fellow, Warren Gentry?" shouted Abe across the room.

The lawyer continued acting as if ethics still mattered. "Oh, you must mean Warren Gentry, manager of the local office of the Union Pacific Railroad. He's one of our most outstanding citizen here in Dallas."

Abe stood up. "An' just where might I find this outstanding citizen about now?"

Sensing the Ranger was about to leave, Dolan wasted no time in answering. "It's noon. You'll find him at the Cattleman's Restaurant. He has lunch there every day."

Abe closed the file and left. As he was going out the door, he heard a heavy sigh of relief come from the lawyer. He doubted Mr. Dolan would become involved in anything like this again.

The restaurant was nearly filled to the walls. The man at the doorway stood at a podium type affair, and there was a red velvet-covered book open and setting in the center. He looked up at Covington as he approached and asked, "Do you have a reservation, sir?"

Abe shook his head no, then pulled back the side of his coat to reveal his Texas Ranger badge. "An' I don't need one. Warren Gentry in there?"

Unaccustomed to such straightforward talk, the young man wasn't sure how to answer. "Well, sir, that kind of information—well, our customers, sir, prefer—"

"Dammit boy, just tell me! Is he here or not?"

Abe was beginning to lose patience with all this privacy stuff the people of Dallas seemed so fond of. "Well, dammit! Is he?"

"Uh, yes, sir. That's Mr. Gentry over by the bay window. I'll take you over and—"

"You just stay put and play with your little red book there. I can walk over on my own."

The young man lowered his head and mumbled, "Yes, sir."

Abe removed his hat and made his way across the room. There were two other men in business suits sitting with Gentry. Abe felt uncomfortable in his thirty-dollar suit surrounded by what was obviously the hub of Dallas business society in their expensive clothes and well-groomed haircuts, eating fancy lunches that cost more than a cowhand made in a month. He was definitely out of place in this crowd, but he was determined to make every effort to conduct himself in a professional manner.

"Mr. Gentry. My name is Captain Abe Covington, Texas Rangers out of Austin. I need a few words with you, sir."

Gentry was a man of robust size with a chubby face, bushy eyebrows and muttonchop-style sideburns that Abe hadn't seen since The War Between The States. His attire was of the finest quality and befitting of a man of obviously considerable financial means. Like most people of wealth and influence, Warren Gentry had an attitude as big as his three hundred some pounds. He looked up at Covington in his trail-worn suit and vest and, displaying a slight smirk, waved his fork at the Ranger.

"I can't be bothered with you now, sir. You'll have to make an appointment through the staff at my office. Now run along; these gentleman and I are involved in an important meeting."

Abe saw Gentry's associates grin at one another, and the three continued on with their conversation as if Abe were no longer there. But Abe didn't leave. Again he spoke.

"Sir, this is a matter of such importance that it cannot wait. I'm afraid I must insist."

Shocked, the two men with Gentry stopped eating and placed their forks on the table. Gentry, his face turning a crimson red, suddenly shouted for a waiter.

Practically everyone in the place had stopped eating and was now staring at them. A waiter and the maître d' from the podium rushed over to the table. Gentry pointed to Abe and in a loud and boisterous voice ordered that he be removed at once. The waiter grabbed hold of Abe's arm. The Ranger took one look at the man and said, "You wanta keep that hand, you better move it, friend."

With Abe Covington, a look was as good as a slap in the face, and the man got the message. He quickly removed his hand from the Ranger's arm. Abe leaned over on the table and looked Gentry in the eye.

"Okay, you fat son of a bitch! I tried bein' nice, but you Dallas folks don't seem to appreciate good manners from us backwoods folks, so now we'll do it my way. Get off your fat ass, mister, you're under arrest!"

The dinning room came alive with a flurry of murmuring and whispers. Gentry's face was a mix of surprise and embarrassment as he screamed, "I'll have your badge for this, you bastard. I know the governor personally."

Abe pulled out the letter he had been given by Jacob Olson and waved it in Gentry's face.

"Well, so do I, Mr. Railroad Man, an' this here paper gives me all the authority I need to arrest you." Hooking Gentry under one arm, Abe started pulling the big man to his feet. "Now get off your fat ass—we're leavin' or am I goin' have to roll you through the damn door?"

Humiliated, Gentry couldn't wait to get out of the restaurant. Once outside, Abe led him toward the marshal's office, with Gentry making threats all the way.

"You're going to wish you'd never been born when I'm through with you, Covington. I got friends."

"So do I," barked Abe, "an' one of 'em is out there somewhere right now havin' to run for his life because of you and your damn railroad. You better hope he's still alive, Gentry. If he dies because of what you done, they'll be fittin' you for a pine box."

Gentry's face went blank. "I don't what you're talking about. What man?"

Abe didn't say anything else until they arrived at the marshal's office. Once inside, he set Gentry down in a chair and tossed the wanted poster on the desk in front of him. "Just answer one question. Are you the son of bitch that had that death warrant printed up on John Thomas Law? Yes or no?"

Gentry looked down at the poster and ran his hand through his hair as he muttered, "Oh, good Lord. I told him that this was a mistake." Looking up at Abe, the man said, "This man John Law never had anything to do with that train robbery, did he?"

"No, he didn't. But thanks to you he has most of the state of Texas trying to kill him for that damn ten-thousand-dollar reward. An' for your information, your little poster there's already been responsible for the death of over ten innocent people mistaken for John Thomas Law. The governor and the attorney general are mad as hell over this. That means somebody is going to pay for those deaths, Gentry, and right now that someone is you."

Warren Gentry no longer had the confident look he'd displayed in the restaurant earlier. Right now he was no more than a frightened little man who knew he was in trouble up to his neck and was desperately searching for a way out.

"Now wait. You can't blame me for this. There was a train robbery. Those two girls were killed. That's a fact. You can't deny that."

Abe had already had the marshal gather all the information on the crime. Gentry was right; there had been a train robbery outside Fort Worth on March 3, and five people all told had been killed when a passenger drew his gun in an attempt to stop the holdup. In the gunfight that followed one of the outlaws and four passengers were killed, including the two young women mentioned on the poster. The leader of the gang turned out to be Choctaw Roberts, a sometime member of the Sam Bass outlaw gang. Roberts and six of his men were cornered outside Waco, and all but two were killed by a posse led by a team of Pinkerton agents. They caught one of them. The other man got away. The soul survivor stood trial, was found guilty and hung two weeks later. When the marshal finished reading the report, Gentry set up in his chair and shook his head.

"It was that last man, the one that got away that pushed him over the edge. He couldn't stand it—knowing that one of them was still alive out there somewhere."

Abe pulled up a chair and sat down across from Gentry.

"Whoah, hold it up there, Gentry. What are you talkin' about? Drove who over the edge?"

"Paul R. Tibbets. He's the chairman of the board for Union Pacific. One of the women killed on the train was Lucinda Ann Croswell; she was his daughter. Croswell was her married name. When he heard about it, he went crazy. Tibbets and Allan Pinkerton had been friends during the war. After the funeral, he went to Pinkerton and gave him twenty-five thousand dollars to hunt down and kill everyone that had been involved in the robbery. He had more faith in Pinkerton than in the regular law officers. He figured they would give up after a few days. He wanted them all dead. Pinkerton hired a special team of agents. He instructed them that there were to be no trials, no jury, no chance that any of them might get prison sentences. Of course, he'll deny that if you ask him."

"They almost got the job done," said Abe.

"Yes, they would have succeeded if it hadn't been for some of your Rangers. They showed during the fight and took one man into custody. There was nothing the Pinkerton men could do. Some of the Pinkertons wanted to shoot it out with the Rangers, but fortunately cooler heads prevailed."

"So five were killed that day, one hung later and one got away," said Abe.

"Yes, you would think that would have satisfied him, but it didn't. He became obsessed with the one man that got away. He kept pressing Pinkerton to find him, but they had no idea who they were looking for. The one man they caught refused to give them a name. One night they placed an agent in a cell next to the man. Over the period of the trial the agent gained his confidence. The night before he was to hang, the man admitted that the man that had shot the women and gotten away was a gunman named John Thomas Law."

Abe shook his head. "So this agent gives Pinkerton the name and he gives it to Tibbets."

Gentry nodded. "Yes. But I wasn't convinced. Neither was Pinkerton. He proved that by refusing to go after the man. No amount of money would change his mind. That was when Tibbets came up with idea of the poster. I told him it was a mistake. There was no proof of anything the condemned man said, nothing. But he wouldn't listen. He had me write up the posters, get them printed and distributed, then put a lawyer on retainer to pay the reward. Now what I was afraid would happen has happened. But why would a man tell such a lie knowing that he was going to die the next morning?"

Abe reached up and took the file from the marshal. He flipped through a few pages then stopped. "Damn," he muttered as he read the name of the man that had been J.T.'s accuser.

"Ricardo Williams."

Gentry looked over at Abe. "You knew the man?" he asked.

"Damn right I did. Him and his two brothers were wanted for rape, murder and robbery. Come from a Anglo/Mex marriage. All three boys mean as rattlers. Killed their father with machetes, hacked the poor bastard to death. John Law tracked them down and killed two of 'em. Ricardo got away. Guess this was his way of paying Law back for his brothers. Still, someone should have checked him out before printing up these posters."

Gentry nodded in agreement. "I know, Ranger, but hell, he didn't give up the name until just before they hung him. That was good enough for Tibbets."

"Where can I find this Paul Tibbets?" asked Abe.

"He runs our main office in Kansas City."

Abe stood up to leave. Gentry asked, "What's going to happen to me, Ranger?"

"I don't know, Mr. Gentry. That'll be up to a judge to decide. Like I said, a lot of folks have died because of this here poster, an' I reckon there'll be a few more before it's over. Somebody ought to pay, don't you think so?"

The man sitting alone at the desk now was a mere shell of what he had been earlier. Gone was the look of power and arrogance. It was a frightened, humble man that did not answer, but simply nodded his head up and down in agreement as the Ranger walked away.

Abe and the marshal were talking in front of the office.

"Guess that clears John Law. But there's still the matter of those three men he killed escaping from jail in Santa Angela," said the Dallas lawman.

Abe lit a cigar as he replied, "I already got some men down there working on that."

"What are you going to do about this fellow Tibbets?"

"With any luck at all, J.T.'s still alive and we can find him. If he is, I think it's only right that he go with me to Kansas City to arrest Tibbets. I'm sure he'll want to meet the man that caused all this trouble."

Abe went to the telegraph office and sent two messages. One was to Jacob Olson requesting a warrant for the arrest of Paul R. Tibbets. The other was to Ranger William Tyler, informing him that he had discovered the name of the man responsible for the wanted posters and that his arrest was pending. He was returning to Austin. If John Law could be found, he was to meet him there.

ELEVEN

✦

J.T. AND THE Rangers arrived in Santa Angela just
before sunset. As they rode into the livery to stable
their horses, Pablo come running in from the corral.
There was a big smile on his face as he saw J.T.

"Ah, my friend, the saints have been good, you are
still alive."

Pablo's smile suddenly faded as he saw the gunfighter grimace in pain as he dismounted, holding his
side. Hurrying to Law's side, Pablo draped an arm
around his neck and helped J.T. to the bench along the
wall. Once he was seated, the old man lifted the corner
of J.T.'s shirt and looked at the wound.

"Don't worry, friend. It looks worse than it is. Just
painful that's all," said J.T.

Pablo smiled again. Grabbing a bottle of his brother-

in-law's special blend of tequila from behind a feed
sack, he removed the cap and held the bottle out.

"I have just the thing to take away the pain."

John Law grinned. "If it'll peel the paint off this
barn, I reckon it can make me forget this hole in my
side."

Law took a long, hard pull on the bottle. His eyes
started to water as the harsh liquor burned its way
down his throat. He'd been right about one thing—it
damn sure made a fellow forget any other pain he was
having.

Billy led his horse into a stable, tossed his saddle on
the sidewall, then joined J.T. and Pablo at the bench.
"Pablo, have you seen Ranger Overby today?"

"*Sí, señor.* He had been keeping the eye out for Señor Turnbolt as you told him, but no one has seen the
mayor since yesterday. Some say he may have already
run away. But I don't think so. My cousin, she is a
maid at the mayor's *casa.* She says that Señora Turnbolt has left for Austin to visit her sister, but that nothing has been taken from the mayor's closets, no clothes
or luggage for a trip. He is still here, but no one knows
where. If not in town, perhaps one of the surrounding
haciendas."

"How about that Captain Westmore?" asked J.T.

"No, *señor.* He has not been in town since they arrested you." Looking at Sergeant Towns, he continued,
"But he has released Señor Reeves and his friends from
the jail at the fort."

Towns stepped forward. His face a mask of growing
rage. "What!"

"*Sí,* Señor Towns. They say that there was much

shooting going on that day. No one can say who shot the soldier. The captain say it could just as easy have been Señor Law that killed him. He also say there would be an investigation, but that until then, Señor Reeves and his men were free to return to their homes."

"That son of a bitch!" shouted Towns. "He's made another deal, this time with Reeves. For what? I have no idea. But somethin' ain't right here."

"You got that right, Sergeant," said Billy. "Damn, J.T., you're the only one we been able to find since we got here. We have no idea where this Turnbolt fellow is. Hell, we couldn't even find that waitress down at the café."

This news caused J.T. to sit up. "What? Pablo, where's Rita?"

The old man shook his head. The worry was clear in his face as he said, "I don't know. I told these Rangers I would try to find her when they went to search for you. But just like Señor Turnbolt, Rita is nowhere to be found. The café, they say she went to see a sick friend. She was to be gone an hour. No one has seen her since. I ask around all her friends; none of them are sick. None have seen her. I do not know, *señor*, I just do not know."

The tequila must have worked. J.T. got to his feet. He didn't feel any pain.

"You're right, Sergeant. Something ain't right here. The mayor's missing, his wife suddenly goes to Austin, now Rita is missing too, and we got Reeves and his boys roaming around out there when they ought to be in jail. The whole damn thing stinks to high heaven."

Ranger Overby came running into the barn. "Billy,

we got company. Looks like a bunch of bounty hunters to me. Someone told 'em we had John Law in here. You better get down there an' talk to 'em. Way they figure it, only thing standin' between them and ten thousand dollars is three guns with Ranger badges."

"Damn!" said Billy. "That posters got 'em comin' out of the woodwork."

"Yeah," said J.T., "an' I'd bet you my saddle it was Harry Reeves that told them I was here. Well, let's go see how bad these boys want that money."

Billy stepped in front of J.T. "Hold up, John T. We done left plenty of bodies out there in the sands around Fort Graham. We don't need no more. Let me talk to these fellows before we start shootin'. Once I tell 'em there ain't no reward money they might ride on."

Big Mike frowned. "How many are they, Tom?" he asked.

"I counted ten," came the reply.

J.T. shook his head. "No, Billy. I ain't lettin' you fellows fight my fights for me. We were lucky out in them dunes. Things might not work out as well this time. I'm goin' with you."

Big Mike and Tom both nodded in agreement. "He's right, Billy. When they see they'll have to go against the three of us and John Law, they might just change their mind. You can still do your talkin', but if they start somethin', I want this man with us."

"What do you think, Sergeant?" asked Billy as he turned around.

Lincoln Towns wasn't there. He had slipped out the back door while they were arguing. The men looked at one another as Big Mike said, "Damn, I never figured that fellow for the runnin' kind."

Pablo pulled an old muzzle-loading musket from behind one of the stables. "I will fight beside you my friends."

J.T. took the ancient weapon from the old man and set it aside. "No, Pablo. We appreciate the offer, but if you really want to help us, go to the Mexican part of town and see if your people have any news of what has happened to Turnbolt and Rita. We'll take care of the rest. Now go, but be careful, my friend."

Pablo nodded and disappeared out the back door. The four men checked their guns and walked out the double doors to the front. As they moved down the street, Billy reminded them all, especially J.T., that he wanted to talk to the bounty hunters before there was any shooting. They reluctantly agreed. As they neared the main street, they saw the line of horses tied off in front of one of the saloons. Three of the new arrivals were standing on the boardwalk and saw them coming. One leaned inside the saloon doors and called out to the others that they had company coming. Within seconds, the other seven men appeared. The group stepped off the walk and out into the street to face the lawmen.

"We ain't got a chance in hell," said Tom Overby.

"You're right," said J.T. "But we'll give Billy his chance to talk anyway."

Billy stopped forty feet from the men. Reaching into his pocket, he withdrew the letter the attorney general had given to him. J.T. recognized four of the men in the group. They had crossed trails before during their hunts for wanted men, had played cards and drank together before moving on. It seemed strange that they should now be facing each other in what could well be a fatal last encounter.

"Who speaks for you men?" asked Billy in a strong, confident voice.

They looked around at one another then motioned for one of the men J.T. recognized to do the talking for them. As the man stepped out in front of the group, J.T. suddenly recalled his name. It was Charlie Bowdine.

"Howdy, Charlie," said J.T. in a friendly tone.

Bowdine nodded as he moved forward. He saw the blood on the side of Law's shirt and pants. "John T. Looks like you've had a rough go of it."

J.T. smiled at the tall, well-built man with the tied-down gun.

"Yeah, I've had better days, Charlie, that's for sure. Billy, this gentleman's name is Charlie Bowdine. Charlie, this is Billy Tyler, Texas Ranger out of Austin."

Billy took a couple of steps closer and held out the paper signed by Olson.

"Mr. Bowdine, if you and your associates will take a moment to read this letter from the attorney general, I think it'll clear up a lot of confusion that's going on around here about a certain wanted poster involving Mr. Law."

Bowdine took the paper and stepped back into the light from the saloon. A few of the other men gathered around him as he read the letter. When he had finished, the men whispered among themselves for a while, then Bowdine came forward and handed the paper back to Billy.

"How do we know that letter's real," he asked, "an' not just a trick you Rangers cooked up to get John T. out of here and back to Austin?"

"I can assure you this letter is real, Mr. Bowdine. It was given to me by Jacob Olson himself three days ago in Austin. J.T. Law is innocent of any crime in the state of Texas. The wanted poster that is out on him is not a legal warrant. It was not issued by the state of Texas. We are trying to find out who is behind this. My captain is in Fort Worth right now meeting with this lawyer, Dolan. But there is no reward. There is no need for trouble here tonight."

"What do you got to say about this, John T.?" asked the big man.

J.T. looked at the faces among the group of gunmen as he spoke. "Charlie, you know me. Do you really think I would shoot two women? What the Ranger says is the truth. I only found out about this thing a few days ago myself. All I got to back that up is my word."

Charlie thought about that for a moment then, grinning, nodded as he replied, "Got to admit, I thought there was somethin' funny about that flyer when I saw that about the women. But seein' numbers that big can cloud a man's mind sometimes, John T. You know how it is. You always been a fair man. As far as I'm concerned, your word's good enough."

This brought a wave of grumbling and whispered cussing from some of the men behind Bowdine. The big man looked back over his shoulder then back at the lawmen.

"You got me convinced. But I can't speak for the rest of these boys."

Bowdine turned around and raised his hands to quiet the men. "You fellows pushed me out here to do the talkin' for you. Well, I done heard enough to convince me that I had a long ride for nothin'. I believe what the Ranger says. Those of you that know J.T. Law know he don't lie and he damn sure wouldn't shoot no woman. Myself, I'm goin' inside, have a drink, then head back to Dallas. I'd suggest that you boys do the same, but if you still ain't convinced, well, you just go on an' do what you think you gotta do. But I'm out of it."

Bowdine walked through the group of men and into the saloon. Three others shrugged their shoulders and followed him inside. The remaining seven whispered among themselves for a minute, all the while casting threatening glances at the lawmen.

"What do you think, J.T.?" whispered Billy.

"I don't know, kid. I don't know these fellows. At least the odds just got better."

The seven men began to spread out across the width of the street.

"Ah, hell," uttered Big Mike, "this ain't good."

Once they were set, one of the seven shouted, "We don't want no fight with you Rangers, but we aim to have John Law with us when we leave here. So step aside and you won't get hurt."

Billy was quick to answer. "Reckon not, boys. You want him, you're goin' have to take him after we're dead."

Big Mike spit, then said, "Guess that means we're done talkin', huh, Billy."

"Spread!" said J.T.

The lawmen and J.T. had begun to put some distance between them when one of the seven yelled out, "There won't be a one of you bastards standin' when this is over, by God!"

Suddenly there was the sound of guns being cocked as hammers were pulled back. But none of the men in the street had made a move. A voice from above the men shouted out, "You got that shit right, mister!"

The men all looked up to see Sergeant Towns and two squads of Buffalo Soldiers lining the rooftops on both sides of the street. They were aiming their heavy caliber Sharp's rifles at the seven bounty hunters. The sound they had heard was the hammers of the big guns being cocked back. Black fingers now rested on triggers awaiting the order from their sergeant to fire.

"Jesus Christ! They're everywhere," said one of the men, who quickly threw up his hands.

"Now real slow, you boys lose them gun belts. If even one of you gets stupid on me, you're all gonna die. Now let 'em drop—now!"

"You heard the man," said a nervous voice among the seven. "Don't nobody get stupid. Drop the damn gun belts."

Big Mike and Tom Overby rushed forward and quickly collected the weapons.

"Corporal Jefferson!" shouted Towns from atop the hotel roof.

Jefferson and two other troopers came racing on their horses and halted them in the middle of the street. "Yes, Sergeant!"

Towns rested his arm on his knee as he looked down and said, "Jefferson, collect those weapons and escort

these seven gentlemen out of town. Remove all the
bullets from the guns and the gun belts. Once you're a
fair distance out, give them their guns back. Gentlemen, I'll say this just once. You come back here, I'll
have you all shot on sight. Move 'em out, Jefferson."

The Rangers watched as the troopers got the men
mounted and followed them out of town. J.T. was the
first to greet Lincoln Towns when he came down off
the roof. Taking the man's hand in a firm grip, he
laughed as he said, "Seems like savin' my ass is be-
comin' a full-time job for you, Sergeant Towns.
Thanks again."

A wide smile crossed the man's face. "Well, when
Mr. Overby said there was ten of 'em, I figured you
wouldn't mind a little help."

Tom Overby slapped the sergeant on the back.
"Now, I like this man's idea of a 'little help.' "

"Yeah, thanks, Sergeant. That business could have
got out of hand real quick if you hadn't showed up,"
said Tyler.

"I'm surprised he let you out of the fort," said J.T.

Towns smiled. "Guess I forgot to ask his permission,
Mr. Law."

"So what do we do now?" asked Big Mike.

His voice weak and holding his side, J.T. replied,
"We try to find Rita and that bastard Turnbolt."

It was apparent to all present that John Law was in
no condition for an all-night search of the town. He
was still weak from the loss of blood and needed to
rest. It was only after a heated argument with Billy and
the others that the bounty man finally relented and al-

lowed himself to be taken to a room in the hotel and a bed. There wasn't really anything they could do until morning anyway, and they were all tired. They would get a night's rest and start out fresh in the morning.

TWELVE

✡

THE MORNING STARTED off hot and miserable and went downhill from there. The problems began when a Mexican boy came running into the stables looking for the Rangers. He was sweating, out of breath and speaking so fast no one could understand what he was saying. Billy managed to calm him down long enough to learn that Pablo had been found shot and lying beside the road outside of town. The boy wasn't sure if he was dead or not. The people that had found him had taken him to the doctor's home and sent the boy to fetch the lawmen.

"Mike, you better go get John T. He'll want to know what happened. We'll be at the doc's house," said Billy.

Mike didn't say anything. He strapped on his gun

belt and ran out the door for the hotel while the boy led Tyler and Overby to where Pablo lay wounded and dying. When they entered the room, they saw the grim look on the medical man's face. Pablo lay on a table, his body covered in blood. The doc worked feverishly trying to stop the flow of blood from the numerous holes in Pablo's chest and side. He had been hit broadside with a shotgun blast. The Rangers had seen a lot of shotgun wounds, but this was one of the worst.

They heard the front door swing open and hit the wall as Mike and J.T. came into the room. Tyler saw the pained look in J.T.'s eyes as the gunfighter looked down at the old man. A sadness came over his face as he leaned down and ran his hand through the old man's hair. Pablo was a hard man; his fists were clenched and he bit his lower lip as the doctor probed the open wounds, removing piece after piece of buckshot from the frail old body. He was shaking violently and there were tears in his eyes, but he never uttered a sound.

"Who did this, Pablo?" asked J.T. as he took a rag and dabbed at the sweat on the man's forehead.

Pablo opened his mouth to speak, but only blood came out. He began to cough, then choke on his own blood. The doctor dropped the probe and quickly pulled him upright. This brought a scream of pain from the old man. But the doctor had no choice; if he didn't sit him up, he would choke to death.

"Get behind him," shouted the doctor. "Hold him up at an angle. We got to keep that blood from blocking his airway until I can get this damn bleeding stopped. God, what a mess."

J.T. and Big Mike stood behind the table using their

bodies to prop the wounded man up. Law knew he was in terrible pain, but they had to know what had happened.

"Pablo, was it Turnbolt?"

Pablo shook his head from side to side.

"Reeves!" said Billy.

Pablo nodded that it had been Harry Reeves, then moaned in pain as the doctor cut into the side of his chest in an effort to find the source of the internal bleeding. The smell of blood filled the small room. The young boy that had led them there grabbed his stomach and ran out of the room. He was going to be sick.

"Did you find Turnbolt or Rita?" asked J.T.

Pablo nodded his head up and down. He then reached out and grabbed J.T.'s hand and held it tightly.

"Goddammit! You got to hold him still!" shouted the doctor.

Pablo tried to speak again. "*Casa,* Rosa" he uttered. "Rosa. They are there. Mayor has Rita. Holding her there. Reeves, going to kill, kill, them all."

Pablo's body shook again and a stream of blood spewed forth from his mouth, covering the doctor in red. Tossing his scalpel to the floor, the man wiped the blood from his face and shook his head. "I'm sorry. There's nothing I can do. There's massive bleeding. I'm sorry."

Pablo's grip tightened around John Law's hand. His old eyes looked up at him.

"Rita, please, you save her, my friend. Please."

J.T. started to answer, but before he could speak, Pablo took in one final deep breath—his chest rose, then slowly fell. The life had gone out of Pablo Vargas.

J.T. reached out and gently closed the old man's eyes. The room that had only moments ago been filled with anxious shouting and a flurry of activity was now quiet. The only sound was the praying of the old women in the outer office. Big Mike lowered Pablo down on the table. He removed his hat out of respect, as did the others in the room. After a silent moment of prayer, the doctor ushered the men out of the room. He told them to go on and do what they had to do. He would take care of the arrangements for Pablo.

Outside the house, J.T. called over the young boy that had gotten sick. He asked if he knew of a woman named Rosa and where she lived. The boy was still shaken by the horrible sight he had seen in the house, but he nodded that he did. He could show them where it was. As they followed the boy down the main street, J.T. told them to wait a minute. He ran inside a saloon. When he came back out, he was carrying a sawed-off double-barrel shotgun. Rejoining the group, he shoved extra shells into his shirt pocket, and they again began walking to the end of the street and into the Mexican section of town.

As the men moved down the narrow streets four abreast, women grabbed up their children and rushed them into their house, shutting the doors and the window shutters behind them. Old men playing dice at open-air tables in front of the cantinas saw the men coming and left their games for the safety of the walls inside the bars. Many had no idea what was going on, but from the manner of their walk and the grim looks on their faces, they knew these gringos were looking

for someone, and when they found them there would
be a fight.

The boy came to the end of a street and stepped up
next to a wall. Looking at J.T., he pointed to a row of
adobe houses across the street and told him that Rosa's
house was the one with the shirts hanging on the line
in the front yard. J.T. gave the boy a twenty-dollar gold
piece, thanked him, then told him to leave.

Breaking open the shotgun, Law checked the loads
in both barrels then snapped it shut. Looking at Billy
Tyler, he asked, "You want to do any talkin' here,
Billy?"

The young Ranger shook his head. "Not this time,
J.T. Talkin's over."

"My feelings exactly," replied Law. "Overby, you
and Big Mike go around to the back. We don't know
who all's in there, but be careful if the shootin' starts.
There could be two women inside. Me and Billy are
going through the front door. I'll give two minutes to
work your way around, then we're going in."

The two Rangers nodded that they understood, then
began working their way around the building and to
the end of the row of houses. They disappeared behind
the one on the far end and slowly moved from house
to house until they were directly in back of the one the
boy had pointed out. Taking up positions behind a
woodpile, they aimed their guns at the back door and
waited.

"You ready, Billy?" asked J.T., cocking back the
hammers on the scattergun.

"You got the cannon. You lead the way."

Both men stepped out into the street and straight up

to the house. J.T. raised his foot and kicked the door open and both men ran inside. Two men sitting at a table eating grabbed for their guns but never had a chance, as fire leaped from both barrels of the shotgun, blowing the table apart and the two men with it. Three more men were standing around a bed in the corner of the room watching a fourth man raping a woman. Startled, two of them went for their guns while another ran for the back door. Billy fired four times, hitting both men twice. They were slammed up against the wall and slid to the ground dead. The man on top of the woman was struggling to get up but his pants were down around his ankles and he tripped and fell. Billy stepped over him and placed the barrel of his gun against the man's forehead. He lay perfectly still. There was the sound of gunfire from the back of the house, then silence. A few seconds later, Overby and Big Mike entered the room through the back door.

J.T. hurried over to the woman on the bed. His first thought was that it was Rita. But he was wrong. This was an older woman. It was Rosa. Her face was covered in bruises and there was blood coming from her nose and mouth. Big Mike found a cup and dipped some water from a bucket then took it to J.T., who now sat on the bed and held the woman's head on his lap. As J.T. held the cup for her to take a drink, Big Mike pulled a blanket off the floor and covered the naked woman. Then he pulled the man Billy was holding at gunpoint over to a wall and told him to stay put.

Across the room in another corner, sitting in a pool of his own blood, was the body of Ernest Turnbolt. He had been cut to pieces and his throat slashed.

"I take it the little man in the corner here is Mayor Turnbolt," said Billy.

"Yeah," said J.T.

Pushing back a floor-length curtain to reveal the body of another man wearing a suit, Billy asked, "Then who is this fellow?"

Rosa pushed the cup away from her mouth, and as painful as it was for her to speak, she uttered, "That is Señor Ballard, the banker man. He brought money for Ernesto this morning." She began to cry. "They killed them both—my Ernesto and the banker."

Billy knelt down and checked the body. "They cut his throat too."

"They used knives. Gunfire would have attracted too much attention," said J.T. as he dabbed at the blood around Rosa's busted lips. "Was Rita here, Rosa?" he asked as he gently continued his work.

She nodded slowly, "Yes. They took her with them."

"What was she doing here, Rosa?"

She explained that Turnbolt couldn't be seen so he had her send a boy with a note to the banker telling him when and where to bring the money. She had told the boy that she was too ill to take it herself. Rita must have talked to the boy and, believing her longtime friend to be ill, had simply left work to come and check on her. When she found Turnbolt there, the mayor had no choice but to hold her until he and Rosa could leave town. He had tied her up, but never intended to harm her. She would be able to free herself after they had their money and had left.

"But then, they came," said Rosa as she broke down and began to cry again.

J.T. tried to comfort her as he asked, "Who did this, Rosa?"

"Señor Reeves and his men. They burst in and he began yelling at Ernesto and beating him."

"Why, Rosa? Why would Reeves be angry at the mayor?"

"I do not know. Señor Reeves, he spoke the name of the Army captain at the fort a number of times, but I did not understand what that had to do with us. Ernesto begged them to stop, but they kept beating him. When I pleaded with them to stop, they hit me, hit me many times. Then his men, they began to rip my clothes. They threw me on the bed and they—they started raping me. They made Ernesto and Rita watch as they took turns."

Big Mike and the other men in the room cursed under their breath and lowered their heads or looked away. There was nothing lower in Texas than a man that beat and raped a woman. J.T. could feel her body tremble as she told the story. He squeezed her hand.

"It's all right, Rosa. No one is going to hurt you anymore. The men that did this will never hurt another woman. I promise you that."

She wiped the tears from her eyes and caressed the back of his big hand.

"Ernesto and I were lovers, you know. Oh, he wasn't a big man in size maybe, but when those men began doing those things to me, he tried to protect me. He broke free from the men holding him and struck Señor Reeves in the face. That was when Señor Reeves cut him the first time. Then the others drew their knives. They formed a circle and began pushing Ernesto around

the circle, cutting him on his arms, his face, his chest.
It was a terrible thing to watch. Rita screamed for Señor Reeves to stop his men, but he only laughed and
struck her with the back of his hand. Some wanted to
rape her, but he would not allow that. That was when
Señor Ballard arrived. The poor man had no idea what
was going on. They pulled him into the room and began stabbing him. The money belt he had brought for
Ernesto fell to the floor. Señor Reeves picked it up.
When he saw the money, he laughed, then simply
reached out and cut the banker's throat. When Ernesto
called him a bastard, Señor Reeves drove his long knife
into Ernesto's chest. Rita tried to run away, but there
were too many of them. They caught her. Señor Reeves
told some of his men to take her out the back door. He
then told those you killed here, when they had finished
their fun with me, to cut my throat like the others and
join them."

She paused and squeezed J.T.'s hand again before
saying, "They were about to do that when God sent
you and your angels to save me from these evil men."

"When did Reeves and the others leave, Rosa?"
asked J.T.

"Not long before you came. Maybe twenty, thirty
minutes. I am not sure. I am sorry."

J.T. rubbed her hair softly. "No, no, Rosa. That's
fine. Don't worry. We are going to find those men, and
when we do, we are going to send them all to hell."

"Amen!" said Big Mike from across the room.

Billy came over and knelt down by the bed.

"Rosa, did you hear them say where they were going
or where they were supposed to meet these other men?"

She shook her head. "No, señor, they no say."

J.T. eased himself off the bed, laying Rosa's head on a pillow.

"You're asking the wrong person, Billy," he said as he crossed the room to where the survivor rapist sat against the wall. The man's eyes were wide with fear and he was shaking all over as J.T. knelt down beside him. His eyes were cold and threatening as he said, "You know where they are, don't you?"

The man was so scared he couldn't talk. His lips were quivering as he shook his head from side to side and quickly averted his eyes downward. A sadistic grin began to form at the corners of J.T.'s mouth.

"Sure you do. Reeves told you boys to catch up to them when you were through having your fun with the woman. You know where they are and we both know it. Maybe you just forgot. Or maybe you didn't hear the question."

The man drew his knees up to his chest. His eyes darted around the room at the unfriendly faces staring down at him. They wanted to kill him; he could see it in their eyes, especially the man kneeling in front of him. J.T. reached over in the corner and pulled the bowie knife from the mayor's chest. Holding the bloody blade upright in front of the man, he slowly turned it in his hand, and his menacing voice spoke again.

"Maybe I can help you remember."

The razor-sharp blade flashed out and down so fast that those in the room weren't even sure they had seen it happen. The man against the wall flinched. His hand shot up to the right side of his head, clutching at the sudden unexpected pain he had felt. He then stared in disbelief at J.T.'s left hand J.T. was holding the man's right ear between his fingers.

"Sweet Jesus!" muttered Overby as he stared at the severed flesh.

The man wanted to scream, but fear had gripped his throat, and instead, he let out a sorrowful moan. Tossing the ear into the middle of the floor J.T. switched the blade to his left hand.

"Maybe you can hear me better now. Where did they take the girl?"

The man brought both hands up to protect his left ear. The blade flashed again, this time the man screamed out in pain as the razor-edged blade severed his left thumb, leaving it dangling from his hand, held only by a slim sliver of flesh. The man's hands came down. He grabbed his left wrist with his right hand. In an instant, J.T. inserted the point of the blade up one side of the man's nose and slashed outward cutting it wide open. The man screamed again and began to cry.

Slowly turning the blade in his hand again, J.T.'s cold eyes stared at the man withering in pain.

"Don't cry on me, you son of a bitch. I ain't even started on you yet. Now where's the girl?"

Billy stepped forward. Looking down at the sobbing man, he shouted, "For god sakes man, tell him what he wants to know."

"Go on, fellow," said Overby. "You don't owe them bastards nothin'. Hell, you know they musta heard them shots, but they left you anyway, didn't they?"

The man stopped crying and with pitiful eyes looked up at J.T.

"If I tell ya, will ya let me go? Ya won't kill me?"

J.T. lowered the blade of the knife and let it slip from his fingers. The heavy blade dropped straight down and stuck in the floor at the man's feet.

"No, I won't kill you. Where are they?"

With the agony of the pain he was feeling clearly in his voice, the man answered, "We was supposed to meet out at the old Swinson place. That's where we'd be paid our money."

"What money?"

"The money for helpin' kill Turnbolt. Reeves said we'd get paid after the job."

"By who? Captain Westmore?" ask Billy.

"Honest to God, I don't know. It could be the captain. Reeves met with us in his office before they let us go. I don't know the details, but Reeves said we could all get clear of that killin' of the nigger soldier and make some money at the same time if we went along."

"What about Pablo? Who shot him?" asked J.T.

The man seemed confused by the question. "Don't know nothin' about that. We never shot nobody. Reeves left us for a while early this mornin', said there was somethin' he had to take care of. Coulda been him. One of the boys thought he saw some ol' Mexican guy in the alleyway when we rode into Mex town."

"An' that's all you know?"

"I swear to God, I don't know nothin' else, mister."

J.T. turned to Billy. "You got any more questions you want to ask?"

"No."

"How 'bout you, Mike? Overby? Anything?"

Both men shook their heads no.

"Then I reckon we're finished here. We'll get our horses and head for the Swinson place. Mike, ask some of those women outside to come in and care for Rosa."

As J.T. started to stand, he pulled the knife from the floor and with one quick swipe of the blade cut the throat of the man sitting against the wall. The surprised look was still in his eyes as he slumped over on his side.

"Dammit, J.T.! You said you wouldn't kill him," shouted Billy Tyler.

J.T. wiped the blood from the knife on the dead man's pants and stuck it in his boot. As he walked by the young Ranger, he replied, "I lied."

While they were saddling their horses at the livery, Sergeant Towns suddenly appeared at the door. He walked up to Billy and gave him a message. Santa Angela didn't have a telegraph office, but Fort Concho did. The wire was from Abe Covington. Towns said it has arrived late last night. Billy read it, then letting loose with a rebel yell he walked up to J.T. and held it out to the gunfighter.

"Abe's found the man responsible for all this, John T. He's on his way back to Austin. Not going to arrest him until you get there. Figured you'd want to be there when he did."

J.T. looked down at the paper in his hand. Good old Abe. He was a friend a man could count on. What should have been a moment for celebration was overshadowed by the morning's events. Harry Reeves and what was left of his men were still out there, and they had Rita. At the moment J.T. didn't feel like celebrating—he was in a killing mood and Harry Reeves was at the top of his list.

"I'm sorry about, Pablo, Mr. Law," said Towns.

J.T. swung up into the saddle. "We all are, Sergeant."

J.T. started to ride out but paused at the open doors. Turning in the saddle, he looked back at the sergeant.

"Towns, I want you to give us about a twenty-minute lead, then go back to the fort and tell the captain that me and the Rangers know where Reeves and his men are and that we're going out in a couple of hours to arrest them for the murder of the mayor and the banker."

A look of concern came over Towns's face. "But if he's the one that ordered the killin', he'll either have to warn Reeves or use my troopers to kill him."

"Exactly," said J.T. "He'll be forced to play his hand all the way out. Make no mistake, Sergeant Towns, I'm going to kill Harry Reeves, but not until he exposes Westmore for the son of a bitch he is. Once he does, we'll let the Army justice system deal with him. Hell, Sergeant Towns, you might get to put those irons of yours on him yourself."

Towns smiled at the very thought of that. "Twenty minutes," he said. "Good luck."

With three Texas Rangers riding at his side, John Thomas Law rode out of Santa Angela. The sleepy little out-of-the-way town that had seemed so insignificant only a week ago had borne witness to more killing than it had known in its existence. But this was Texas. It was still a wild frontier, where death was never far away and could call on you at any given moment. The

seemingly innocent little town had nearly cost John
Thomas Law his life and still might—the day wasn't
over yet. The morning had started with killing, and
from the looks of things it was going to end the same
way.

Sergeant Towns waited until the appointed time then
rode into the fort and reported to Captain Westmore.
The story he told had the desired effect upon the officer. Towns could see the near panic in the man's eyes
when he heard Law was innocent and that he knew
Reeves and his men had killed Turnbolt. Westmore told
Towns to sound boots and saddles. He claimed that it
was their duty to aid the Rangers in their apprehension
of the killers. But Towns knew that was a lie. Westmore wanted to get to Harry Reeves before J.T. Law
or the Rangers had a chance to talk to him. As the
troop was preparing to leave, Westmore reminded the
cavalrymen under his command that the men they were
going after were the same ones that had killed one of
their fellow soldiers. If they refused to surrender, he
expected his troopers to give no quarter. They were to
kill all of them.

Westmore was trying his best to incite his men into
a killing frenzy, in the hope that they would kill Reeves
for him. But it wasn't going to work. Towns had gathered his men together earlier and told of the killings,
the kidnapping of Rita and the rape of Rosa, a woman
they all knew. When he told them of the captain's suspected involvement in all of that, few seemed surprised
by the news. As they prepared to ride out, Captain William Westmore was at the head of what he believed
was his command, but it had already been decided

among the troopers that the only orders that were going to be followed were going to be coming from Sergeant Lincoln Towns.

HARRY REEVES HAD posted guards around the house. The gunfire they had heard as they were leaving town and the fact that the rest of his men had not arrived had him worried. Westmore had told him he would meet him at the Swinson place later that afternoon with papers exonerating him and his men of any wrongdoing in the killing of the trooper in the Brady Mountains. During their meeting at the fort before their release, Reeves had seen how desperate the officer had been to rid himself of any involvement in the whole affair.

Using that point to his advantage, he had pressured Westmore into agreeing to pay him two thousand dollars for the killing. The captain had little choice but to agree to the deal. The money Reeves had taken from the banker, Ballard, had been an unexpected, but welcome surprise. At the moment Harry Reeves had everything going his way. He had plenty of money, with more on the way, and he had Rita and her beautiful body as well.

THIRTEEN

THEY RODE IN from the west, J.T. in the lead. He held them up on the far side of a small knoll and dismounted. Together they made their way to the top and looked down on the Swinson house. They counted seven men outside, all carrying rifles. J.T. didn't see Reeves among them. He was probably in the house.

"How you want to handle this, J.T.?" asked Billy.

"Well, Billy, unless I miss my guess, I'd say Westmore and his Army boys are on the way here right now. I want you and the boys to wait right here and see what happens. That captain can't afford to let Reeves out of here alive, or any of those men down there for that matter. He don't know how much Reeves told them. I'm bettin' he'll want to kill 'em all just to be sure. I'm going to move down around behind the house. I don't see Reeves outside; he's probably inside with Rita. I want that son of a bitch to myself."

Billy started to protest, but J.T. cut him off. "No, Billy, that's the way I want it. You boys can cover me from up here. Once the Army gets here an' the shootin' starts, you can join in with them, cut off anyone that's trying to make a break this way."

"They spot you before you get in that house, you could be in a bad way in a hurry."

J.T. grinned. "I ain't worried, son. Remember, I seen how damn well you Rangers can handle those long guns. I'd say I was safer than them boys on the porch down there. You just do it my way this time, okay, Billy?"

Reluctantly, Tyler nodded. "Okay, John T. Watch yourself down there."

J.T. smiled, slapped the man on the leg, then moved back down the knoll and circled around to the left. Ten minutes later, Billy and the others saw a figure moving out of the trees toward the rear of the house. Two guards suddenly came around a corner of the house. J.T. went to ground behind a pile of firewood. The two men walked right by him and around the other corner.

"Damn, that man's got more lives than a cat," said Big Mike.

Overby looked back to the east. "He was right. Here comes the cavalry."

The Rangers watched as Westmore brought his men on line then had them dismount. They moved into the trees and started toward the house. Billy expected the captain to shout a warning for the men to throw down their guns and give up, but that didn't happen. The

captain had no such intention. Once they reached the
tree line, Westmore dropped to one knee and fired his
Colt Army pistol, killing one of the men on the porch.
The fight was on. Gunfire erupted from all around the
house. Two troopers, caught off guard by the captain's
first shot, were still in the open when he fired and took
the brunt of the rifle fire from the porch. They both
went down in a heap. One was wounded, the other
dead. That was all it took. The troopers yelled and
opened fire on the Reeves men. The Rangers added
their rifle fire, and from their high position above the
house they were able to pick off the men too well con-
cealed for the troopers to get a good shot at them.

Hearing the first shot fired, J.T. rushed to the back
door and pushed his way inside. Just as he had expected, Harry Reeves was standing at the window looking out. When he heard the door burst open, he turned
and fired wildly in J.T.'s direction. The bullet tore
splinters from the door frame above John Law's head.
Rita was in the corner; her hands went up to her face
as she screamed. J.T. leaped forward and hit the floor,
firing as he fell. Reeves cried out as a bullet tore
through his leg just above the knee. He fell. Both men
were down. They both fired again at the same time.
Reeves missed; John Law didn't. His bullet caught the
man square in the chest. Reeves let out a loud moan
as the gun fell from his hand and he toppled over next
to a table.

J.T. stood up and moved to where Rita was huddled
in the corner. She was shaking. Reaching down, he
took her hand and pulled her to her feet. Running his
hand through her raven hair, he took her in his arms

and held her tight as he whispered, "It's all right now, Rita. It's over."

She was sobbing as she said, "He killed Grandfather."

"I know. I was with him when he died. He loved you. He wanted me to tell you that."

She broke into tears again. All he could do was hold her.

Outside, the gunfire had stopped. Westmore's plan had worked. Every one of the men outside the house had been killed. As he and his men moved in on the house, he was surprised to see John Law and Rita walk out the front door. At the same time, Billy and the Rangers rode up into the front yard. J.T. had the money belt in his hand. He saw the worried look on the captain's face as he asked, "What about Harry Reeves? Is he in there? Is he dead?"

J.T. didn't answer. Ignoring the officer, he tossed the money belt to Sergeant Towns. "See to it that gets back to the bank will you, Sergeant?"

Towns caught the belt in midair and nodded, all the time watching his commanders' face, which was slowly turning red. Westmore was not accustomed to being ignored.

"I asked you a question, mister," barked Westmore as he took a threatening step toward J.T. He still had his Army colt in his hand. He started to bring it up.

J.T. moved Rita aside, and letting his hand drop down next to his holster, he stared down at the captain. "You don't wanta do that, Westmore."

"Is Reeves alive or dead? It's a simple damn question. Answer me!"

"Yes, he's dead. But he didn't die right away. He told me the whole story. I believe the army is going to be very interested in hearing that story, Captain," said Law with a smile.

Westmore was beside himself. He didn't know what to do now. Of course it was still his word against that of a gunman and bounty hunter. But what if they believed him?

Westmore ran up the stairs and into the house. He had to see that the man was dead for himself. Big Mike brought J.T.'s horse and one for Rita. When they were mounted, J.T. looked down at Sergeant Towns.

"Well, at least this time you didn't have to save my ass, Sergeant. Of course, we did appreciate the help."

Towns reached up and shook hands with the bounty man. "Anytime, Mr. Law. Anytime."

"We'll head back to town now. I'll write up a report about the captain's involvement in all this and bring it out to the fort. Reeves told me everything before he died. You might want to get a wire off to the colonel, tell him what's happened."

Towns nodded and assured him he would do that as soon as they got back to Fort Concho. The Rangers thanked the men of the tenth for their help and fell into line beside J.T. as they started back for Santa Angela. Billy said, "It's a good thing Reeves talked before he died."

J.T. shot him a look that showed a half smile. But he didn't say anything.

Billy looked hard at J.T. then shook his head. "Don't tell me, I already know. You lied, right?"

Before J.T. could answer they heard a voice yell out, "No, Captain!" then there was a shot.

They turned in time to see Westmore drop a rifle and clutch his chest. The man then fell over and tumbled down the steps, landing at the feet of Sergeant Towns, who stood there with his gun in his hand. Captain Westmore was going to shoot the only witness against him in the back as he rode away. Or so he thought.

Towns waved for them to go on as he shouted, "You owe me, John Law!"

J.T. laughed and waved back as he muttered, "Damn, if he didn't do it again."

As they rode on, Big Mike looked at Billy and Overby as he said, "Didn't I tell you? More than a damn cat."

The sound of laughter from the two Rangers could be heard back at the house.

LEAVING THE RANGERS to straighten out the details in Santa Angela, J.T. had Rita pack some belongings and they left right away for Austin. He thought a trip to the big city would do her good and help ease the loss of her grandfather. There was still the business of the man who had put out the wanted posters to begin with. Abe had said he would wait for him before making the arrest. J.T. didn't want to keep him waiting long.

Getting them a room in the finest hotel in Austin, J.T. left Rita to enjoy a warm bath while he went to Ranger Headquarters. He received a warm welcome from Abe as he came through the door. Billy had wired the details of what had happened and told him that J.T. and "a guest" were on their way. Pouring them both a drink, Abe sat across from his friend. When he had given J.T. a few minutes to relax and enjoy his drink, he told him the story of Paul R. Tibbets. When he had finished, he waited to see what J.T. had to say.

He didn't have to wait long. "Well, I'm sorry about the man's daughter an' all, but when do we leave for Kansas City, Abe? I don't know whether I'm going to shoot the son of a bitch or beat him to death."

Abe shook his head. "You're not goin' do either one, John."

J.T. suddenly leaned forward and slammed his glass on the Ranger's desk. "The hell I ain't, Abe. You know how many people been killed because of that crazy old man? Oh, no, Abe. He don't get no free walk on this. I done went through hell and too damn many good folks have died. He's got to know about that."

"He knew, John T. Believe me. He knew."

"What the hell are you talkin' about?"

Abe took a telegram off his desk and handed it to J.T. The bounty man read it, then placing it back on the desk, sat back in his chair, took a sip of his whiskey and stared out the window.

Paul R. Tibbets, chairman of the board for the railroad, had hanged himself some time after midnight. They found a number of newspapers scattered about the floor beneath him. They each contained stories of innocent people that had been mistaken for John Thomas Law and been shot. One of those innocent victims killed had been a thirty-three-year-old man named Robert Tibbets—Paul R. Tibbets's oldest son.

THIRD IN THE
TEXAS BOUNTY HUNTER SERIES

BY TOM CALHOUN

TEXAS TRACKER:
THE LAREDO SHOWDOWN

When his niece is kidnapped, a Ranger
Captian employs the services of J.T. Law.
But finding the mountain cutthroats won't be
easy—and won't be pretty either.

0-515-13404-X

**AVAILABLE WHEREVER BOOKS
ARE SOLD OR
TO ORDER CALL:
1-800-788-6262**

(B020)

WILDGUN

THE HARD-DRIVING WESTERN SERIES
FROM THE CREATORS OF *LONGARM*

Jack Hanson

B061